Praise for
The Miracle of Small Things

Storytelling at its absolute finest. Guilie Castillo Oriard's superb narrative voice—rich in detail and emotion—transports the reader to a place they won't ever want to leave. A scrumptious and satisfying read from beginning to end!

~ Robin Cain, author of *The Secret Miss Rabbit Kept*

The Miracle of Small Things explores the tensions arising from protagonist Luis Villalobos's many incompatible attractions: professional success, beautiful women, loyal dogs, the lure of the coral reef, his own destiny, and his temporary island home of Curaçao. This lovely and compelling book has an enormous heart, pulling the reader along with Villalobos as his problems grow and solutions fade. The stakes are high for Luis as he finds himself deeply entangled in paths that will lead him to a final, difficult choice.

The Miracle of Small Things lavishes praise on its extraordinary island setting, dogs' steadfast love, and human spirit's need to find its own rhythm. Curaçao is lovingly rendered, past and present, as a character itself—post-colonial, starkly beautiful, and captivating. You cannot read this book without checking airfares to Curaçao.

~ John Wentworth Chapin, author of *Alexandrite* and founder of *52/250 A Year of Flash*

Luis Villalobos's life in Curaçao is stretched to the limits of understanding what is important to his soul in thirteen strong short stories strung together as he adjusts to the demands of his job, the relationships he builds, and life on the island. Come along for the ride but fasten your seatbelt; it can get bumpy. And finally, be aware of contemplative hummingbirds, suggesting you do the same about your life. *The Miracle of Small Things* is a five-star read.

~ Rick Bylina, author of the Detective Stark series, including *One Promise Too Many* and *A Matter of Faith*

The combination of money and sex always creates an irresistible dynamic. Add more than a few dogs to the mix, and Guilie Castillo Oriard has created a tale as beguiling as the seductive ambiance of Curaçao itself.

~ Peggy Vincent, author of *Baby Catcher: Chronicles of a Modern Midwife*

Guilie Castillo Oriard has the ability to transport the reader to exotic locales and introduce them to people as familiar as family.

~ Michele Riccio, author of *Ursula: Then and Now*

A richly enchanting story of lives and loves unfolding against the backdrop of the Caribbean, *The Miracle of Small Things* is an enthralling novel in stories written with beautiful intensity, a book of dreams and desires, and a journey to self-discovery that gives life meaning.

~ Silvia Villalobos, author of *Stranger or Friend*

Five stars. Urbane and utterly charming, Luis Villalobos is driven by ambition to become a General Manager of an offshore, international investment firm. His only obstacle to achieving his dreams seems to be his manipulative and seductive boss. And then practical Luis takes in an abandoned dog, his integrity is challenged, and he falls in love.

The Miracle of Small Things beguiles the reader with a witty and compassionate portrait of a year in the life of Luis Villalobos in tropical Curaçao, where nothing is quite what it seems, and all can be lost or gained in a summer afternoon on the beach. Told deftly, with humor and insight into our very human vulnerabilities, this lovely novella by Guilie Castillo Oriard builds upon that quest for happiness we share, a sense of belonging, and makes me want to travel south to find my own miracle.

~ Beth Camp, author of The McDonnell Clan books, including *Standing Stones* and *Years of Stone*

Quirky and wholly engaging, the book sizzles with the heat of the Caribbean sun, revealing consequences of various life choices and renewing readers' perspectives on their own lives.

~ Jeanette de Beauvoir, author of *Asylum*

Written in Guilie Castillo Oriard's typical rich voice, with details the reader can all but taste, *The Miracle of Small Things* proves that sometimes a man cannot be open to finding what he really needs until first he lets go of everything he thought he wanted.

~ Cindy Dwyer, author of *My Roots Are Showing*

The Miracle
of
Small Things

Guilie Castillo Oriard

TRUTH SERUM PRESS
Adelaide, Australia

First published as a novella, August 2015.
Versions of chapters 1 to 12 originally published as part of
2014 A Year in Stories by Pure Slush Books, 2013 – 2014.

ISBN: 978-1-925101-73-7

Truth Serum Press
4 Warburton Street
Magill SA 5072
Australia

Email: truthserumpress@live.com.au
Website: http://truthserumpress.net
Truth Serum Press catalogue: http://truthserumpress.net/catalogue/

Front cover photograph © Loredana Bejerita
Author photograph © Miguel Russo Hart

excerpt from *The Love Song of J. Alfred Prufrock*
by T. S. Eliot © Esme Valerie Eliot

fragment from *Por Mujeres Como Tú* lyrics by Fato (Enrique Guzmán Yañez)
© 1998 Discos Musart S.A. de C.V.

Also available as an eBook
ISBN: 978-1-925101-74-4

For Cor —

Without whom none of this
would exist.

(Yes, literally.)

Contents

◆

Curaçao's is a prickly kind of beauty.

Rough around the edges, camouflaged in the humdrum,
the unremarkable, even the unappealing. It's a rare beauty,
sudden and abrupt; the beauty of a cactus flowering
in the wild, blooms of impossible grace hidden in thorns
and the tromp l'oeil of shadow in the blazing sun.

It's the kind of beauty that, like the cactus flower,
lives in total ignorance of ostentation.

The kind that the traveler seeking glamour
or sycophantic perfection will
never be able to see.

◆

The Miracle of Small Things
January 1st

There's no stillness like the stillness of Curaçao on New Year's Day. Pointless tropical sun on deserted asphalt, every business shuttered, everything forlorn. Not even trash stirs: the wind is on furlough too. There's also no New Year's Eve like Curaçao's, which explains the stillness. But to Luis Villalobos, this desolate emptiness feels like the cold shoulder of the world.

Luis has just ruined his life.

He brakes for a red light even though his black Wrangler Rubicon Jeep is the only vehicle in sight. He's seen no one, not even on foot, since pulling out of Milena's carport. It all feels surreal, like an alternate dimension he's crossed into by accident. In a sense it is: Curaçao is utterly different from Mexico City, London, Hong Kong, anywhere else he's lived.

But he isn't here by accident.

He was lured to this tiny speck of land no one in the civilized world can or wants to find on a map, away from the plum job he'd landed at the legendary Cabrera y Machado law firm in Mexico City, by the one-in-a-million carrot of taking over as Managing Director of Ehrlich Fiduciary's Curaçao branch next year, when the current MD moves to greener fields of power and influence at the Singapore office. Fields which make Luis salivate, and which, with Curaçao as a trampoline, he would've eventually conquered for himself. Luis's ambitions know no limits.

Apparently, however, his intelligence does.

He could've had his pick of sexy inebriated females last night; they all seemed to find him irresistible. Stepan told him to enjoy it, that new-kid-on-the-office-block popularity. "You single, right? Go for it, bicho. Won't last forever." And, wearing his new colleague's permission like a groupie brandishing a backstage pass, Luis did go for it. With Milena Durant, the Managing Director of Ehrlich Fiduciary's Curaçao branch.

The boss.

The woman he's supposed to replace.

Luis taps his forehead against the steering wheel—softly; a headache is already barreling down the helpless conduits between neurons. Even with the car's A/C at full blast, he catches whiffs of Milena's Carolina Herrera.

In this world Luis inhabits, the world of financial planning and asset management, where profit justifies not just means but every low trick in and out of the book, there is only one taboo: sex with a colleague. That's the sleaze line. Sex with the boss—well. Professional hara-kiri, just not quite so swift.

He runs his tongue over his teeth and checks the light. Still red. He craves a toothbrush. A shower, with a Karcher high-pressure cleaner. Then he'll scour the internet for plane tickets, make some quiet inquiries. Perhaps Cabrera y Machado will take him back. His fast track to a partnership will be gone, of course, but he'll work 24/7 to earn it back. He'll offer to take on the Compliance division, the one no one wants because of the constant government liaison. He'll take it on, he'll make it thrive, he'll be the hero. And he'll get his partnership back. It can be done.

Details of last night, all blurry and inconsistent edges, swirl out of the cotton in his head. The dancing—salsa. Jesus. No other woman came close after that spectacle. Later, at the beach bar, Milena on her knees in the sand rolling up his pants. They walked under the moon and the fireworks until she stumbled, they fell into the surf, came up drenched and sandy and laughing and—kissing. "Let's dry off at my place," she said.

Even through the haze of all that beer, he saw the seductive glint in her eye. No innocent lamb to between-the-sheets slaughter, him.

The traffic light blinks, turns orange. He missed the green, dammit. He steps on the clutch, the gearshift grates—anyone might think he's never driven a stick before. The Jeep lurches, catches, finally rolls across the empty intersection.

Last night was a test, and he failed. He revealed weakness; hotheadedness, a lack of scruples. No way Milena will endorse him as her successor now.

No. Something's off.

In the three weeks he's known Milena (not counting the afternoon she interviewed him in Mexico five months ago), he's never seen her do anything, no matter how spontaneous it might seem, without calculating to the decimal every consequence. Advantages, risks; all laid out in her flowchart mind like chess moves in Bobby Fischer's.

The self-pitying mini-him argues he's being paranoid. The Mexican gentleman in him is aghast at blaming the girl. But his gut feels the spot-on pang of truth. Last night wasn't just a test, wasn't just premeditated. It was blueprinted.

Luis marks a right turn, then a left. The *tck-tck-tck* sounds exactly like the clicking of his father's eternally disappointed tongue. *You've been had, chamaco.*

He pokes at the remote on the sun visor. The Warawara Resort gate swings open with a silent faltering, second-guessing itself. He shoves the gearshift into first, burns rubber shamelessly on the climb into the parking lot.

On the walkway to his condo, he fishes in a pocket for his keys with a chuckle of grudging respect. Ah, Milena. She owns him now. No wonder she looked so smug standing in her kitchen this morning, wearing his shirt. And he was so

15

flustered, couldn't even find the words to ask for the shirt back. He fell for it, all of it. Well, she better enjoy her moment. He's taking the first flight out, cutting those puppet strings.

Where the hell are his keys? He clearly remembers them in his hand—when? Not today. Last night? Oh. At Milena's. He thought he was following her to *his* place, tried them on her front door until she giggled and handed him a Montblanc keyring. "Maybe this one?" It worked, and he pondered that for what felt like an instant but must've been longer because then he was falling on a wide bed and Milena was straddling him, undoing the remaining buttons of his shirt and whispering, "Luigi, I've been looking forward to this."

Luigi. And he felt like Rudolph Valentino while his self-esteem—and his keys—fell to the carpet, unnoticed.

What does she want?

There's a spare of the patio doors hidden in the bougainvillea by his pool. He cuts through the alley of chalkstone chips between his condo and the neighbor's, giant-steps up to the deck with knee creaking—and stops short.

There's a monster in the patio. Black, gigantic, sinister—although this last tones down when the monster wags its tail. *Thump-thumm-thumm-thump.*

Luis falls back to the pebbles. "Fuera. Shoo."

The monster opens its maw, rolls out a too-pink tongue. Panting. Like a grin from the Big Bad Wolf.

"Shoo. Go on." Luis claps, and in the silence it sounds like a gunshot, but the only effect is a speeding up of the tail. Thumpathumpathumpa.

He picks up a handful of stones. Damned if he's going to let a dog manipulate him, too. But the monster's tail plunges between his legs and he skits away with a very un-monster-ish whimper before Luis lets fly the first stone. Black eyes, frightened but also hurt, pine at Luis from across the pool.

16

Out of the patio's shade and in the sun's glare the monster has become a skeleton: protruding hip bones, ribs so marked Luis can count them—and the vertebrae above them.

Luis steps up to the deck. "Sorry, guy. I wouldn't've—"

The dog cowers, backs away, never takes his eyes off Luis.

"Look." Luis raises the hand with the pebbles, slowly, and with a chalky clatter releases them to join their kin on the walkway. "See? No more rocks."

Is that a twitch at the tip of the tail?

"Dude, stop. I don't need a guilt trip."

The twitch this time is unmistakable.

Steps crunch in the alley. Vikram, the neighbor on the left, ducks into view from under the palm trees bordering his yard and hollers, "Marjan! That dog is back!" Then he sees Luis. "Oh. Hey, is that dog yours?"

Luis will never know what he would've said because Marjan, Vikram's Dutch wife, calls out in her nasal whine from their porch, "I'm calling Animal Control again."

"Wait."

Vikram looks Luis up and down. "It's yours then?"

Luis glances at the dog. He'll tell himself later the eyes did it. In them he sees—imagines he sees—a plea. "That's right."

Vikram purses his mouth and studies the moment. "You need to take better care of him."

Great. Now he's a dog abuser.

But Vikram smiles before disappearing back into the palm trees. "I know a good vet," he says with a wave. "I'll get you the number. Happy New Year, neighbor."

"Thanks. Uh, you too." Luis turns to the dog. "I just bought you some time, bud. Now scat."

The dog sits up and cocks an ear.

"You want to end up in the pound?" The dog shakes its head and Luis laughs. "Have a good life, dog."

But the dog stretches instead. The gesture looks ingratiating, almost flirtatious.

He's never owned a dog. Ma's allergies meant no pets. Later, living alone, he never had time. Not that he does now. Besides, he's leaving. Like, tomorrow.

Going back home, his own tail between his legs. Begging for his old job back. Giving Pa the satisfaction of another *I told you so.* They say decisions are choices between consequences. Compared to Pa, Milena is a beast he can tame. Who knows, maybe he'll teach her a thing or two about puppeteering himself. Or not. His arrogance has been known to get him into trouble. On occasion.

He can leave anytime. Doesn't have to be tomorrow. He could wait, see how things play out. Buy Mr. Loch Ness over at the edge of the patio some time, maybe find him a home.

"What do you think, bud? You want a home?"

The tail twitches again, more sure of itself.

"Domestication's a bitch, man. You realize you'll need a bath."

The twitch becomes a full-out wag.

"Shots, too. And there is absolutely, under no circumstances, any peeing inside the house."

More tail wagging.

Luis laughs. "Don't even know what you're agreeing to, do you?"

That panting wolf-smile.

"All right, then. Here, bud. Come on. You got to let me touch you."

◆

The concept of treaty shopping started in Curaçao
(and Switzerland).

In 1955 the tax treaty between the Netherlands and
the US was extended to include Curaçao. The island
could now route investments in American companies
without paying tax in the US. Many took advantage of this,
including Americans—which, after a while,
the IRS did not find amusing.

The treaty extension was rescinded in 1988,
and offshore profits in Curaçao plummeted:
USD 225 million in 1985, USD 62 million in 1998.
By 2012, only 10% of the island's income came from
the offshore sector.

But Curaçao has a long history of adapting, not just
to survive but to thrive.

◆

The Chablis and Sushi Miracle
February 1st

Just past 10:00 am Luis Villalobos walks into the lobby of
Ehrlich Fiduciary with a thick binder in one hand and a
hazelnut cappuccino in the other. He's already a regular at
the Barista place, even though it means a detour. Given this
island's appalling lack of choice, though, good
cappuccino—strong, the foam thick enough to chew—is
worth any sacrifice. Mornings like today it might warrant
arson. Or murder.

In the elevator he takes a grateful sip and squares his
shoulders for the mirror. He didn't shave, and his hair is still
wet from the shower. At least it's gelled and combed. His
shirt is untucked, sleeves rolled to just above the elbow. But
he looks better than he feels. Between the files and Milena's
wine, he slept maybe an hour.

On the third floor he waves at the other die-hards.
Wendolyn of course, the head of the LatAm team. She's
there every Saturday, even some Sundays. Julissa, her
assistant, nods from the printer room. Stepan, Legal
Counsel, lifts a royal hand from his corner office opposite
the hall from Luis's.

"Ciao, bicho."

Luis opens the door wider. "Jesus, Stepan. You
experimenting with cryogenics in here?"

Stepan sits back and his chair creaks. "Blasted heat.
Every morning I consider suicide. Or a transfer to
Luxembourg."

Luis sets the binder on Stepan's desk. "I vote Luxembourg. None of this bullshit there."

"Nowadays? Everyone has US investments. No escape from FATCA."

"But in Luxembourg—anywhere, actually, except here—they know that due diligence means, at the very least, getting proof of tax residency from clients." Luis jiggles the binder, a little tap-dance on the desk.

Stepan looks out at the Caribbean morning glittering outside. "When I started here—I'm talking years, not decades—dude could come in off the street with a driver's license and a suitcase of money, and we'd set up an investment structure for him. Any trust company would."

"The good old days. Right." Luis presses his eyeballs until fireworks bloom under his lids. "Stepan, OECD directives started back in the seventies. How did you people slip under the radar?"

"The whole Caribbean did. How?" Stepan snorts. "Isn't it obvious?"

"Offshore may mean unregulated, but not sloppy. This," Luis makes the binder dance again, "is sloppy. Negligent, even."

"Well, then." Stepan peeks over his wire-rimmed glasses at Luis. "Isn't it lucky Ehrlich has you. Tackle one of these a week, I'd say you're fully booked for the next, oh, five years."

"We don't have five years. Ehrlich or me. The FATCA deadline is April."

"And that's why you've been taking these fat ladies home with you, you nasty fetishist. So did, uh—" Stepan pulls the binder around with one finger so he can read the label neatly pasted on its spine. "Almeida NV put out last night? Or did you just rip her bodice of fiduciary malfeasance and rape her?"

"Whoever set up those trusts raped the client and he doesn't even know it."

"I think it's a she. What trusts?"

"The three trusts that act as shareholders of Almeida. They're—well, maybe not straight-out sham, but close. They're all revocable. Invisible trustees. The beneficiary has powers of attorney for the bank accounts, and there's bank accounts everywhere. Name the jurisdiction, Almeida has an account there. No statements, no transaction info of any kind."

"Sounds like a textbook case of sham to me."

"And yet, Counselor, you're not worried."

Stepan leans back in his swiveling chair, stretches both arms up above his prematurely balding head. "Faulty structures are our daily bread, bicho. I mean that literally. Fixing them brings in good revenue."

"Fixing them takes time. Which we don't have."

"Because of the FATCA deadline? That's only for Curaçao entities. Most of those ducks are in military parade formation."

"The subsidiaries of those ducks are relevant to the FATCA audit, Stepan. We have to disclose, which means *they* need to be in military whatever, too. Or we resign before April."

Stepan studies Luis. "You discussed this with Milena, did you?"

Luis feels his armpits dampen, even inside Stepan's little corner of the Arctic. He meant to bring it up last night, but Milena had a different agenda. "She'll agree. It's a win-win for everybody."

"Especially the IRS," Stepan says, blue eyes twinkling.

"Why? No US persons are involved."

Stepan blinks at him.

"Stepan. Fuck. I thought that was policy here. No US persons as clients."

"Without proof of tax residency, how can I—or anyone—assert that?"

"See no evil?" Luis's stomach is on a wild ride.

Stepan chuckles. "Plausible deniability. Cheer up, bicho. Wendolyn and her troops will swoop through the Curaçao files well in time for the deadline, and then we'll start due diligence on the others." He rubs his hands together, a gourmand at a banquet. "I went through two of Core Tech NV's subsidiaries last night, and I found some interestingissimo shit. Look at the assessment I left on your desk. Billing's going to go through the roof this year. You'll be a hero. Not a bad start to your career with Ehrlich, eh?"

Luis thought he'd seen the smutty underbelly of the financial world during his stints in Hong Kong, Guernsey, Wall Street. They're all heaven, compared to this. Here, in the cradle of the trust industry, it's just a step up from the abacus. From quills and inkwells, a cowled monk recording transactions in spiky longhand. At least there's computers.

While his boots up, Luis swigs the last of his now-cold cappuccino and flips through Stepan's report.

Source of wealth declaration says inheritance. But where's the backup? No will, a faded death certificate, copy of a copy, and not notarized. An Ehrlich certification stamp on a corner, initials scrawled over it. He turns the page to decipher it. M. D. Ah. It figures.

An hour later, when MD herself—Milena Durant and, how germane, Managing Director—pops into his office, he's turned Stepan's three pages into a twelve-page litigation dossier.

"Good morning, Luigi. Again."

He gives her the least belligerent smile he can manage. "Sorry I left so early. I had to—"

"Don't. I hate excuses." She saunters in on six-inch slingbacks, pointy things with red daisies fragile enough to be made of glass, certainly too fragile to carry Milena's curves. She sits a thigh on the corner of his desk, pushes the to-do tray away, leans over the report. It's on purpose, all of it: the skirt riding up, the twist from the waist so her ass looks rounder and her cleavage shows just enough swell. He knows this, and still that non-discriminating entity between his legs twitches in appreciation. He glances across the hall, but Stepan has his back to them.

"This is wrong, Luigi."

"Sloppy, yeah. And negligent."

But Milena is giggling. "No, honey. This one," she points to a triangle in the structure diagram, "Almeida N.V. That's the only entity domiciled in Curaçao. All the others aren't. The audit doesn't include them."

"They're part of the client's structure. We need to—"

"No. We disclose what we're required to disclose. We do not volunteer information."

"But—"

She grazes his cheek. "You didn't shave."

"Milena, listen. FATCA isn't a game. Once Curaçao signed that exchange of information agreement, all fiduciaries operating under a Curaçao license are bound, by law, to provide the declarations—"

"And we will. But the request is for entities domiciled in Curaçao. Until the US Treasury learns to widen the scope of their requests, we provide only the information they ask for. Not a goddamn byte more. Are we clear?"

The upbraiding stings like a bitch slap. "Yes, ma'am."

She puts a palm back on his cheek, ignores the bristle this time. "Don't pout. I'm just training my replacement."

He subdues the impulse to recoil. "Is it official?"

"That I'm leaving next year? I already signed the Singapore contract."

"That I'm your replacement."

Milena's red mouth purses. "Potentially. Is that enough?"

Luis trails a finger over the contour of her knee. "For the moment."

"A threat?" But she's laughing. "If you don't get to be MD you'll—what? Leave?"

"There'd be nothing to stay for."

"You could come to Singapore."

He laughs too. These things are best approached disguised in humor. "As your lapdog? Enticing."

She tweaks his ear, a tad too hard. "Speaking of. How's the monster mongrel?"

No trouble smiling for real this time. "Dog food is bankrupting me."

She turns away, fiddles with his computer, clicking through the open programs. "Take him to the shelter, Luigi."

The feel-good lasted all of three seconds. Maybe Milena does it on purpose. It bothers him that she might know him well enough already to play emotional yo-yo like that. "Nah. We're good, Al and I."

Her laughter is sharp, the one she uses with novice account managers. "Does he call you Betty?"

The Paul Simon association never occurred to him. Creatively challenged as he is, he'd planned to call the dog Bud. Then, for reasons he doesn't think about much, a fragment of poetry started looping in his head as he drove to the vet that first time. *Let us go then, you and I / When the evening is spread out against the sky.*

One more thing Al can be grateful for. He could've spent the rest of his days answering to Pru. "It's for Prufrock," he tells Milena. "You know. The Love Song of J. Alfred."

"Whose song?"

He almost says the lines out loud. Suddenly he doesn't want to share it, another piece of his soul for her to play with. "An old poem. Doesn't matter."

"Isn't poetry wasted on a dog? Seems to me your Pure Frock might be better served recited to me. Over Chablis and sushi on the beach? I have a bottle cooling in the car. You get the sushi?"

If he had a tail, it would be expected to wag. "I've got hours to go here."

"But I just cut today's workload by——" She glances at the structure diagram. "By five. Come on, it's too beautiful a day."

"One condition."

She's already at the door. "No Al, Luigi."

Luis thinks of the dog's forlorn face when he leaves, the joy when he comes home. But this due diligence project is the key to getting out from under Milena—figuratively and otherwise. "No, no Al. But hear me out on the FATCA thing. You're right about the scope of the request. But we need to get those subsidiaries in shape, Milena. Ehrlich can't function, not anymore, without proper due diligence. For every entity, every client."

Her lacquered fingernails tap against the pressed wood. "Just this once. And you promise to never bring it up again. In public or private."

"Just—hear me out."

A Chablis and sushi miracle. That's what Luis needs.

◆

The magic of Curaçao is in the details—and the island's
reefs are the perfect example. There's plenty of big stuff:
dolphins, turtles, tarpon, moray eels, rays, mantas,
even the occasional shark. But it's the tiny
that makes diving here unique.

The seahorse swaying to the tide's tango tempo
in the shallows. The hair-breadth shrimp of electric blue and
fluorescent orange body. The miniature perfection of coral,
and the underwater-fireworks display of coral
spawning under a full moon.

It takes time to train your eye to see past the large, past the
spectacular, to the tiny bursts of color, the ethereal fragility.
To the miracle of it all, teeming, just below the surface.

◆

Dive
March 1st

Under the palapa roof of the school's terrace, the dive instructor with ridiculous sun-bleached curls is bringing the briefing to its merciful end. Luis Villalobos swallows a caustic cheer. He'd be in a better mood if he'd stopped at Barista for a cappuccino, but there was barely time to shower before Wendolyn showed up.

He sneaks a look at her. Like the other two diver wannabes at the picnic table, she's hanging on each of the instructor's words, simpering like a groupie.

The instructor—Jan from Amsterdam, which rhymes pronounced the Dutch way, the stress on the *dam*, the short *a*—rubs his hands in a bad imitation of a wicked witch. "Let's check if you've been paying attention. What's the first rule of diving?"

"Keep blowing bubbles!"

Luis's knee jiggles under the table impatiently. He—Wendolyn, too—should be at the office. Milena seems pleased with the results of the FATCA project so far, but she expected nothing. She had to be wrestled in, and now she's broadcasting each success to the Ehrlich mothership in Singapore as if it was all her initiative. She won't be so eager to claim credit a month from now, when Ehrlich's credibility is in shreds before the US Treasury.

No. A month from now it'll all be on Luis.

But it's Carnaval. The halls of Ehrlich Fiduciary stand deserted. His FATCA task force is otherwise engaged:

teener parade, children's parade, main parade, costumes, rehearsals. He laughed at first, until Marco from HR sat him down and explained about this most sacrosanct of Curaçao celebrations. And so, exasperated, he let Wendolyn rope him into being her buddy today. *Buddy*. Next he'll be best *pals* with Jan from Amsterdam.

"All right!" Mr. Amster*dam* claps once and gets up, nods at the six-foot-eight dive master on the terrace steps. "Guillaume will get you your gear."

"You excited?" Wendolyn brushes his arm as they fall behind the giant Guillaume. Her judicious flirting is still subtle enough to be ignorable. Luis hopes, somewhat ruefully, and mostly for her sake, that it stays that way.

The other two novices, an American couple on their honeymoon—who takes a diving course on a *honeymoon?*—save Luis from lying. "Totally excited," the girl says, and tugs on her child-husband's arm. "Aren't we, Robbie?"

"Stoked, man." Robbie grins at Luis. "You?"

Luis rolls out a smile, more charity than irony. "Totally stoked."

"Hey, Luis?" Jan pronounces it Louise. An improvement; usually he gets Loo-is. "Hold up a sec. You look a little out of it. You okay?"

The possibility of honorable discharge looms. But Wendolyn's still within earshot, so he says, "Yeah. No, I'm fine. Just—late night."

Jan looks him over, nods. "Drank a lot?"

"Ten, twelve beers." He had eight.

Jan flips through the medical histories on his clipboard. "You smoke, huh? But no cardio history, no back problems, no regular headaches. Except for now?"

Luis obliges with a chuckle.

"You in good shape? Physically?"

Luis shrugs, nods.

"Fifty push-ups, soldier."

Hope rises. He'll never make it past five.

Jan chucks him on the shoulder. "Kidding. But stay close to me, understand? Your eyes, on me, all the time."

"Actually—" Luis glances toward the equipment shack, where everyone has crowded around Guillaume like Lilliputians around Gulliver. "I'm not feeling so hot. Maybe it's best if I—"

"You gonna go chicken on me, man? It's just an intro dive. You'll be fine."

Guillaume approaches, holds up a pair of boots. "You are 11, yes? Try these booties."

Booties?

The rest of the equipment comes with grown-up names. Wetsuit—XL, because the L felt like medieval testicular torture. A buoyancy control device, which Guillaume and Jan call BC—Luis hates shoddy acronyms—that hinders everything, protects nothing. The dive master tugs at three of the hundred straps on the vest-like thing and decrees, "It fits." Flippers—more straps. Mask—another strap.

So that's that. Luis is expected to survive underwater in boots, a wetsuit that—regardless of what size the tag says—still feels too tight, and an inflatable lifesaver that requires more assistance than Marie Antoinette's corsets. As a plot twist, Guillaume tucks four two-kilo metal blocks into the thing's pockets.

"Guillaume will assemble your gear today." Jan stands over the giant kneeling on the sand in front of six tanks, each a tad smaller than the dive master's thighs. "Intro courtesy only. If you sign up for the course, you'll learn how to do it yourselves next time."

No next time for Luis, and for that he feels immense gratitude.

Short-lived. "Luis." Jan is crooking a finger at him. "Over here."

Guillaume holds up a tank with Luis's BC strapped to it. Jan parts the snarl of nylon and velcro to reveal an armhole of sorts. He adjusts and clasps and clicks Luis into place. "How does that feel?"

Luis wriggles his shoulders. "Like a straitjacket."

Jan snorts. "You been in many of those? Guillaume, let go of the tank."

The vest tightens against Luis's shoulders and stomach. "Ooof. No, it's good." He hates that he sounds so strained.

"Pussy," Jan says with a wide smile as he saunters to check on the others.

The walk down the beach to the surf, all twenty steps of it, is purgatory. The wetsuit is hot. The tank bumps the back of his legs. His feet feel clumsy in the boots. The harness velcroed at his waist makes a ripping noise with every movement. The rubber hoses spouting from the regulator, aptly nicknamed octopus, tangle his arms. One hooks up to the BC. Another ends in a gauge with numbers in the thousands that mean nothing to Luis. Two other hoses, one yellow, one black, end in mouthpieces. Jan folds the yellow into one of the myriad BC pockets. Luis fishes behind him for the black one, studies the mouthpiece, turns away from the happy crowd. He hopes it's been cleaned properly. It tastes rubbery. He breathes in, gets nothing.

"Tank is not yet open." Guillaume pats his shoulder, fumbles behind Luis's head. "Oh-kay. Try now again?"

Luis takes a tentative pull, gets a loud life-support sucking sound. And air! Funny-tasting. Dry. Drier than normal, at least. He will never again take that lovely, effortless provision of oxygen for granted.

He's not cut out for this. The only reason he doesn't call it quits is because he's certain he'll never be able to get out of this torture chamber people call diving gear on his own. He's equally certain Jan and Guillaume will be happy to set him free—once they've shown the Three Enthusiasts the marvels of life underwater.

Ocean, finally. The water feels so good on his skin, sautéed in sweat beneath the wetsuit. He dunks his head, soaks off the grumpiness. Taste of salt on his lips. Sound of baby waves kissing the beach. Photoshopped blue of this ocean.

"Inflate your BCs," Jan says somewhere to the left. "Luis! Where you going, man?"

Luis has drifted with the current. He struggles back to where the others are standing in waist-deep water, the weight of the equipment toppling him off-balance if he walks and the tank's nozzle poking a hole at the base of his skull if he tries to swim.

Jan takes hold of his vest and drags him closer. "Remember our deal? With me. All the time." He gropes at the hose on Luis's shoulder. Again the life-support whoosh but somewhat muted. "How does that feel?"

Like the hand of King Kong crushing his ribs. Panic subsides when Luis realizes he now floats without effort. "Good. Yeah."

Jan readjusts straps, checks the gauge, fiddles with the tank, hands Luis the black mouthpiece. "Check your air. Can you breathe?"

Whooooosh. Luis sounds like Darth Vader. Probably looks like him, too. Hard to talk with that thing in your mouth. Luis gives Jan a thumbs-up.

Jan rolls his eyes. "That means up. Get your signals straight."

Right. They covered hand signals in the briefing. Luis makes a circle of thumb and forefinger, the universal OK sign.

"Good boy. All right, everyone over here, please. We're going to do some drills underwater, get you comfortable, then we'll head out to the reef. Okay?"

The Enthusiast Chorus holds up comically identical finger circles. "Okay!"

§

Forty minutes later, six heads bob back up onto the surface. Six faint splashes. The whoosh of six BCs inflating. The pop of six regulator mouthpieces being spit out. Six faces marked raccoon-style from the masks. And the eyes, the telltale eyes: four pairs brimming with the high of boundaries breached.

Luis wriggles his jaw, winces. He must've been clenching that mouthpiece too hard.

Jan is looking at him. Is that a glint of pride in his eye?

Head still full of the great blue below, the thrill of weightlessness (even though Jan had to add four more kilos to convince this lily-livered, oxygen-addicted body to sink), a feeling of having returned, the prodigal child, to a primeval state of grace, Luis grins. Already in love with the pain in his jaw.

"When can we do this again?"

◆

Carnaval in Curaçao is serious business.

So serious, in fact, that it has its own musical genre:
Tumba, a 6/8 rhythm of manifest African roots and clamor
of drums that snatches hips into dance and lips into grins.
The Tumba festival, held several weeks before *Carnaval*,
decides the song that will become that year's *Carnaval*
anthem. And the song's composer, the crowned Tumba
king or queen, attains eternal fame and glory.

◆

The Hunt for Pélagie Solak
April 1st

The inside of Luis Villalobos's Rubicon Jeep feels like an oven preheated for the Christmas turkey, even with the air conditioning at full blast. "Ultra powerful compressor," the salesman said back in December. "Special for Curaçao." Four months later, barely spring, and the island heat has already defeated it.

And Milena has defeated Luis.

As he parks outside the ironwork gate of #74 Jan Sofat, his phone buzzes in the Jeep's central console. Milena. He's tempted to lower the window and throw the damn thing into the mangroves.

How *could* she?

And how could *he* have been so trusting? Like a fool— so apropos today—he'd been celebrating. A year's worth of due diligence work achieved in two months, just in time to meet the FATCA deadline next week. If he had failed, it would have cost Ehrlich Fiduciary its license. And Luis his righteousness, after all the confrontations with Milena.

But he never expected her to pull rank, go behind his back. Or Wendolyn to fall in with it.

He'd brought in a tray of *pastechis* today—cheese, everyone's favorite—to celebrate with the team. Celebrate their achievement. The triumph of his integrity. *See?* he was telling the world—Milena's world, in which he has no desire to live—*It can be done.*

Wendolyn moving the stacks of paper to make room for the *pastechis*. The list catching his eye as she shoves it out of sight. It's an alphabetical list; Almeida NV should be at the top. And it's not. Wendolyn looking at Julissa, her assistant. Julissa looking at the floor. Comprehension beginning to crack wide open. The tray of *pastechis* growing cold. Discovering Wendolyn's true loyalties hit hard, but what hurt most was her justification. *It's just six entities, Luis. Only one is domiciled in Curaçao.* She sounded just like Milena.

He locates a bell next to the gate, rings it twice. Six days to fix this. He'll do it himself. He will, by God, show them all.

A huge uniformed maid is shouting to make herself heard over the barks and growls of the dozen dogs swarming around her in the driveway. "I already said, suh. Miz Solak not home."

"Yes, I heard you. And I'd like to wait for her."

The dogs push bared teeth through the bars in the gate, the whole solid-iron fence rattles, and Luis takes a step back. The maid—Jamaican, judging by how her vowels stretch like putty—smirks. "Could be hours, suh. She have no schedule when she out with the dogs."

Luis eyes the canine Dawn of the Dead swarming the gate. "*More* dogs?"

The maid narrows her eyes. "You not know Miz Solak well, do you? What business you have to see her about so urgently? You selling something?"

"No, I'm not selling anything. It's—confidential. And very, very important."

But he knows he won't make a dent on this Amazon. Besides, he's got a hunch. And an idea. In case it doesn't pan out, though, he hands over a business card. "Would you ask her to call me? Tell her it's important?"

His business card disappears into the folds of the Jamaican's apron. Back inside the sweltering Jeep, Luis makes a note to request heavier paper for his business cards. Something that might provide a full minute of chewing pleasure for a dog.

Weekday car rides mean only one thing for Al. Luis catches him throwing suspicious glances his way from the back seat. "No, bud, no vet. A little work for me first, and I'm hoping you'll help me with that. Then straight-up fun. Sound good?"

Luis heard of this dog beach last month, has been meaning to bring Al. If there's any cosmic justice, he'll find the elusive Solak woman there, no gatekeepers except her dogs. Surely she won't sic them on a fellow pet owner? He ditched the suit and tie at home; without them, she won't suspect who he is until it's too late. He has the Almeida NV affidavit in the glove compartment.

One signature is all he needs.

A dirt road ends at an ocean inlet cradled between the hillocks of the St. Joris valley. A Ford Explorer, red under the mud spatters, is parked next to a burst of mangroves. That's the only sign of human presence—Ms. Solak's, Luis hopes. Everything else is red dust and brambly vegetation. The surf laps at gritty shores with lake-like softness, hardly audible above the bluster of wind that slams the Jeep's door back on Luis's shin.

"Carajo!" He smothers the more violent curses, limps out and opens the back, hooks the leash to Al's collar. "Come on, bud."

Al's front legs are splayed, head hanging low, ears flat. His haunches are quivering. A lamb next in line for slaughter couldn't look more pitiful.

"Nothing to be scared of, man. It's the beach! Lots of room to run. You *like* running. And the water—nice, cool water! It's going to feel so—aw, come on, Al."

Luis tugs on the leash, but Al wiggles back, farther and farther, until he's pressed against the passenger-side door. When Luis switches to that side, Al hunkers away to the driver's side. Finally Luis climbs in, intending to bodily force Al's fifty kilos out of the car.

But the dog's whole body is quaking like a disabling case of Parkinson's.

"Hey, buddy. Hey. What's wrong?"

Al whines, a pitiful, pleading complaint.

Luis cradles Al's massive, shaking body against his chest. It takes several minutes, but finally the dog's trembling is down to brief, sporadic bursts. Luis reaches into the front for his cigarettes. "This wasn't my best idea, huh?"

He lights up in the shelter of the car and steps out.

The pitch of Al's whine shoots up a full octave.

"I'm right here. Just stretching my legs." He lowers all the windows and opens the doors on the downwind side, in the unlikely case Al decides the world isn't as scary as it seems.

"I'd never leave, you know. I'd never—"

The dog, his head so far down his nose brushes the upholstery, is peering out at him.

"Oh. Is that it? Someone abandoned you?"

Al's ear twitches.

"Is that how you ended up a stray, bud?"

But Al isn't listening. Not to him, anyway. Something out by the bay has caught his attention. Then Luis hears it too. Dogs barking. A whistle. He follows Al's gaze and sees six, maybe seven dogs splashing along the shore three hundred meters away. Behind them walks a figure so slight it might be a child. Unless Pélagie Solak is a minor—and according to the file she most certainly isn't—that can't be her. "I'm sorry, bud. I put you through all this for nothing."

The barking pack is driving Al's anxiety attack to a crescendo. Better to leave before they get closer. Luis shuts the doors, turns the ignition, buckles his seatbelt. "We'll try this beach thing again tomorrow, okay? You'll build up your courage, and maybe we'll even get lucky and whatshername Solak will also be—"

A scrabble of nails on upholstery, the Jeep rocks on its suspension, a flash of black streaking toward the bay.

"Al! No!"

Luis forgot about the windows.

His dog is racing for the pack, leash streaming out behind him. Low growling carries back to Luis on the wind.

"Al! Get back here!"

Damn suicidal dog. They'll tear him to pieces. He turns the ignition off, lunges out—shit, the seatbelt. Buckle seems stuck, the band of nylon weave tangles in his arms. Then he's out, tripping over his feet, wishing he could fly. "Al!"

He's not going to reach him in time. Luis watches in horror, legs pumping as if of their own volition, as the pack engulfs Al with a roar.

A whistle, then a single booming HEY!

Luis and the pack—even Al—freeze. The girl—Luis makes out the hint of breasts in the child's tank top—holds up a hand. Like the miracle of bread loaves, her seven beasts, now tame, back off. She approaches Al. The tip of his tail wags. She scratches his chest, takes his leash and, in no obvious hurry, continues her walk around the curve of the bay towards Luis.

With the distance between them narrowing, he's able to make out more details about this dog magician. Small, wiry, no curves worth mentioning. Her face isn't beautiful, not like Milena's or Wendolyn's—no trace of even the memory of make-up, no sexy lips, no come-hither eyes. The skin is freckled, but the bone structure underneath has aristocratic haughtiness. With a shock, Luis realizes this 'girl' is older than him.

The dogs reach him first. He steels himself, but they barely sniff his yet-to-be-broken-in flip-flops before dashing off to the much more beguiling scents his Jeep promises. The woman watches him, waits until she's within arm's length before speaking. "Your dog?"

"Yes." Luis tastes tears in his throat, wants to kick his wimpy self. "Thank you. And—I'm sorry. I didn't—he was terrified, didn't want to get out of the car, and then he suddenly—"

She rubs Al behind the ears before handing over the end of his leash. "He probably thought you needed protecting."

Al licks his hand, looks contrite. Later, in private, he'll crush the dog in the kind of bear hug his dad gave him coming home after a business trip, but in public Luis's macho pride pushes for sassy nonchalance. "Thanks, bud, but I can take care of myself."

The woman doesn't even smile.

Luis wipes the stupid grin off his face, offers a chastised hand. "I'm, uh, Luis."

She looks at it the way one looks at a stale cookie after two servings of carrot cake. Luis gets the feeling she has no qualms of politeness; he won't be the first, or the last, to whom she refuses the honor of her handshake. When she does give her tiny—surprisingly strong—grip, he feels the elation of having been found worthy.

"You risked your dog's life to find me, Mr. Villalobos?"

"How do you know my—"

"Francelle called."

"Who's Francelle?"

The woman smiles for the first time. "You met her at my house."

The ground is cracking under his feet. "*You're*—"

"Pélagie Solak, yes. I didn't realize Ehrlich resorted to out-and-out stalking nowadays. I'll do you—no, I'll do your dog—the courtesy of listening to whatever you have to say. And then you'll do me the courtesy of leaving. Me. Alone. Yes?"

◆

When World War II became inevitable,
Dutch businessmen transferred company seats
to Curaçao to safeguard their assets—and gave birth
to the island's trust and financial industry.

But Curaçao's history as a center of international
transactions began long ago, before even the establishment
of the island's Central Bank in 1828 (the oldest in the
Western Hemisphere). Spanish, Dutch, and British
controlled the island at different times; the natural harbor,
both large and deep, offered prime shelter; major trade
routes intersected here; all contributed to making Curaçao,
in the 1600s and 1700s, a hub for both privateering and the
slave trade. When those were abolished and forbidden,
right on cue oil was discovered in Venezuela and
Shell took over the harbor to build a refinery—which
would provide, along with Jersey Standard in Aruba,
85% of the fuel for Allied planes during WWII.

◆

A Cause for Celebration
May 1st

Luis Villalobos sits in a dark hotel room. The lights of Mexico City spread below, precious stones scattered on black velvet. He loves his city—still his city, even though he's left it behind so often, even though he's lived longer away from it than in it. He loves it, loves its vibrancy, but up here in the tower of the Nikko Hotel he's detached from it, insulated from the cacophony of its streets by the thick glass and soundproofed walls. He'll never be a part of it again, not even when he's down there, in the smog and the crowds and the life. His sinuses haven't stopped aching since they landed. The dry air at twenty-three hundred meters cracks his skin. He grew up here, but four months in Curaçao have changed his pace—of walking, of thinking. No other place where he's lived has done that.

Three days of client meeting after client meeting: breakfasts, lunches, dinners, drinks. A blur of faces and company names and fiscal strategies; of office buildings, security checks, visitor passes; of agendas and proposals and tactful—and not so tactful—reminders of outstanding invoices. Milena packed their week-long itinerary; even today, on Mexican Labor Day, she scheduled six meetings. Thanks to his sinus headache, however, he managed to skip the last two. He's been sitting at the window since sunset.

A knock at the door. He closes his eyes, already mourning the solitude he's about to lose.

49

Knock-knock-knock. One thing Milena won't ever be faulted for is lack of perseverance.

He turns on a light, sets it on low before opening the door. Milena's made-up, dressed-up, and perfumed figure pushes past him. He tries to muster a coat of, if not enthusiasm, at least interest. "How did it go?"

She tosses her handbag and her laptop case on the bed, holds up a Samsonite carry-all with a cocky grin. "They knelt before Zod."

"With offerings?"

She pulls the Samsonite's zipper open like an old-school cabaret stripper and throws him what looks like a very thick checkbook, but isn't. It's a brick of twenty-dollar bills. A Banamex paper strip cinches it around the middle. The bills aren't pristine, but still crisp. A little waxy with the trace of pecuniary fingers.

Milena sits on the bed. "It's only twenty-six K, not even half of what they owe. But it's a start. And they promi—"

"They gave you *cash?*"

"I know, it's inconvenient. But they prefer to avoid a paper trail." She nudges off one black pump, then the other. The soles are bright red. They make Luis think of geishas.

"Milena, we're not dealing meth here. It's our invoices. Corporate directorship, company management. Everything's above—"

"Above board?" She stretches back, reaches for a pillow. "For us, maybe. Not for them. You read the Mexican Fiscal Code lately? Tax planning is a dirty, dirty word."

"Tax evasion's a dirty word. Not tax planning. Which is what we do."

"I love it when you play naïve." She folds her arms behind her head, purportedly to prop it up so she can meet his gaze. She'll have him believe the added bonus of her breasts rising to their best angle is purely coincidental. Her tailored skirt rides up her thighs. The light plays off the sheer pantyhose, highlights the curve of her knee, her calves. But it's the places that remain in shadow that tantalize most.

Luis feels a tingle of pressure at the base of his penis. He turns to the window. "Cash isn't just inconvenient. What, you're going to pack it in your suitcase and declare it at the airport? Wouldn't that defeat the whole avoid-a-paper-trail?"

Not long ago he found her husky laughter sexy. Now it sounds childish; petulant, mocking. "Pack it, yes. Declare it, no. And it's not me, honey. It's *we.*"

He presses a thumb to his left cheekbone, against the pain building in his sinus cavity. "Even if we split it, we'll be carrying more than ten grand each. We have to declare it."

"You're right." She flings herself off the bed to the minibar, whips out a bottle of Victoria beer. "I'll call the client up now, tell them I can't accept their payment because the mighty Luis Villalobos's moral compass is offended by the notion of cash as yet un-sanitized by the alchemy of bank transactions." She slams the fridge door. Its contents clang dangerously inside. "Will that restore your sense of righteousness? The purity of your soul? Or—no, let's just burn the money. Maybe in the bathtub. This is a smoking room, right? The smoke detectors won't know the difference."

"Milena, that's not—"

She skewers the air between them with the unopened bottle. "What is *wrong* with you?!"

Milena in a blazing fury isn't anything anyone needs to experience too closely. Even though without the pumps she stands a full head shorter than him, he takes a step backward. "You know we'd have to declare it. It's the law."

"This isn't about the money. You've been acting like a dick since the FATCA project thing."

He can't hold her gaze, so he looks behind her, into the empty room. "You pulled a shitty trick."

"How many times will we have this conversation? I was protecting you. And I was protecting the success of—"

"I don't need protecting."

"Those six entities had to be omitted from the FATCA list. Don't you see? You would've had a perfect score." She puts her hand on his chest, backs him up against the window and the darkness beyond. "I know my clients, Luigi. The Solak woman won't give us diddly-squat."

The earnestness in her eyes might've swayed him a month ago, a couple of weeks even. "What if you're wrong?"

"Am I?" She leans against him, a mimicry of seduction. "Show me, then. Show me Pélagie Solak's signed affidavit. Her proof of residency. Oh, that's right. You don't have them. And because you decided to put those entities back in the final report, against my express instructions, instead of getting the kudos you worked so hard for, Ehrlich Fiduciary is on the FATCA non-compliant list."

This is news to Luis, and his righteousness trips over it. "I didn't—"

"Mean that to happen?" Milena's face is devoid of any sarcasm now. Even the anger has dwindled. "I got the email this morning. You accuse me of backstabbing, Luis, but you did the same. And then some. Your stupid integrity—"she marks quotations with her fingers—"compromised the entire company."

"Omitting those entities compromised the integrity of the project!"

She turns away, picks up her shoes from the carpet. "That's rich, coming from you. You know why? You don't understand integrity. That virtuous moral code of yours is more full of holes than a golf course taken over by groundhogs. Sex with your boss for personal gain is acceptable, but—"

"It wasn't—"

"—but being loyal to your employer isn't? How do you reconcile that?" She steps into the pumps, fixes her skirt in front of the mirror.

"I've never been disloyal."

"Sshh. She shakes out her hair, finger-brushes it. "Let me tell you about integrity. It's about staying true to the people that matter. You know who matters?" She glances at him in the mirror as she re-pins the chignon. "Our clients. So when your boss—whether you're sleeping with her or not—tells you that excluding a client from an information request by a foreign government is *for the client's own good*, what do you think integrity dictates? That's right. You obey. Because if you don't, you know who will bear the worst of the consequences? Right again. The *client*."

"You just said it was the company that—"

"Ehrlich is in a corner, because you put us there." She picks up her laptop case, slings her handbag over a shoulder. "There's only one way out."

He should've seen it sooner. "We'll have to resign as directors from Pélagie's entities."

"I wonder if you'll still be on a first-name basis with her once she finds out her whole tax structure is going to be dissolved, thanks to you." At the door she pauses, but doesn't turn around. "Take the day off tomorrow. Visit your family, or something."

"But we're meeting with—"

"They were my clients long before they were yours. I can handle it."

When Luis eventually moves, it's only to turn the light off. His head feels like a rotten tomato, all squishy and fragile with the beginnings of remorse. He'll have to go back on his word to leave Pélagie alone. He has to explain, sketch out her options—Milena is wrong, there are options, viable

53

options. He has to help her, any way he can. Maybe she'll even change her mind and sign the—no, careful. Ehrlich resigning as directors is no longer a threat; it's a very near, very real possibility. She needs to understand that. If she perceives it as more coercion, another play to get her to sign the damn affidavit—her adjective, not his—she'll shut him down. He'll never get to speak to her again.

There in the darkness, with the city that he once called home shimmering below him, he finally admits it. He's not feeling remorse. He should, but how could he? This mess has given him the one unimpeachable excuse to see Pélagie again. Why that feels like a cause for celebration is not really clear, but then so little is right now.

The bottle of Victoria Milena abandoned on the dresser is still cold. Luis uncaps it, setting off an explosion of foam from Milena's wild gesturing. He licks the excess from his hand, wipes the rest on his wool trousers—they have to go to the cleaners anyway—and raises the bottle toward the window to toast the night.

◆

For an area of 171 square miles, Curaçao has a lot of beaches. Thirty-eight, officially; and that's without taking into account all the seaside spots too small, or too inaccessible, to make the formal listing.

Most Curaçao beaches are small. No endless stretches of wet sand here; instead, little coves of white sand that the ocean forced open among the cliffs. No Río-like regular rows of towels or lounge chairs; there are too many beaches to choose from, and people like their space.

Loosely gathered groups spread out around the shade of a palm tree or a palapa, or—if beach regulations allow it— around a grill. As the afternoon wanes into mauve and gold twilight, citronella candles will be lit against mosquitoes, a last bottle of wine or cans of Polar beer will make the rounds, and conversation will turn less flighty, more centered...

As it often does under the stars.

◆

When the Sunset
June 1st

The sunset has turned the Caribbean sky into the fire-streaked excess one associates with Photoshop zealots. Luis Villalobos, on a towel by the surf, is thinking about leaving. It's been impossible to get Pélagie alone all afternoon. She's doing it on purpose; she just doesn't give a damn. She's not even angry at him. She's acting like Ehrlich resigning as directors of her companies is the solution to the entire world's problems.

Al is romping with the other dogs, tearing up gusts of sand at the far end of the cove. Chases, gets chased, chases again. Staccato growls reach Luis intermittently, depending on the wind. Part of the game, Pélagie has assured him several times. Indeed, his dog looks as happy and relaxed as Luis has ever seen him. He can stay a little while longer, for Al if not for Ehrlich Fiduciary, or for Pélagie Solak. He can sit here in the orange light, and ponder his defeat.

He hinged, stupidly, his whole career at Ehrlich on this one corporate structure, this one woman. That Luis thought he had a chance in hell of changing her mind, of making her see reason, is living proof of human, specifically male, hubris. Now Ehrlich is at risk, because of her—no, because of him, because of his stubbornness and his sense of integrity, which everyone seems to think is misguided—and the only solution is to cut her loose.

There has to be another way.

He doesn't see Pélagie until she touches a cold beer to the sunburned patch of skin above his shirt collar. "I'm glad you brought Al." She hands him the beer, clinks her own against it in a token toast.

He means to take just a sip—he doesn't need more beer, he has to drive that potholed road back to what passes for civilization on this island—but it tastes so good he downs half in three gulps. "I didn't expect him to make friends so fast."

"They just need time." She bends her willowy body and sits cross-legged on his towel. Her knee bumps his thigh and he moves to make more room. "Sorry," she says, edges onto the sand.

"No, it's—please, sit on the towel."

She pins him in place with those disturbingly clear green eyes that nothing can wriggle away from. "I'm all sandy anyway."

This woman makes Luis feel profane. Around her, anything he says, everything about him, feels like unadulterated crudeness. A tenor pulling out his dick mid-*Turandot*.

"I make you nervous, don't I?"

Away from her gaze—she's looking at the dogs—he's brave enough to chuckle. "Not nervous, no."

"I'm not much good around people."

Luis glances over her shoulder at the crowd gathered around the bonfire. He just met them earlier today, hasn't traded more than a fistful of words with them, but it was enough to know they came—some with dogs, some without and apologetic for it—because Pélagie is here. "Could've fooled me."

She follows his gaze. "Because of them?"

"Seems like a nice group of friends."

"Groupies, really." She smiles, perhaps to take off some of the sting. "They like being associated with me because of who I am, not because of me."

58

Platitudes line up, ready to deploy, but then she says, "Know what I mean?" It's that phrase people tack onto the end of an awkward statement; it's not a real question. But the hell of it is Luis *does* know. He's done it, basked in others' glow—hotshot investment managers, celebrity clients—as if their magic might rub off on him, give him a glow of his own for others to bask in. And how good he felt, how vindicated, when it did. He wants to tell Pélagie there's nothing wrong with an entourage; it's proof of one's worth to the world. But he's afraid it might sound defensive.

"They seem to like you," he says instead.

"They don't know me. They think they do, enough even to judge. But they don't know shit."

Her bitterness startles him. Then it occurs to him he might fit into this category. "Do you think I'm judging?"

She touches the beer to her lips, hesitates before taking a hasty sip. "You think I'm wrong, you're right. That's a judgment."

"I don't mean it to be. I don't, I want to understand, but—"

"And I've explained." She's digging her bare foot into the sand. It's a beautiful foot, weightless and unadorned like the rest of her. "You just don't listen."

"I do." He collects himself, wants to avoid sounding belligerent. "You don't want to be a party to tax evasion. Neither does Ehrlich, Pélagie. That's not what we do. And that's not what your structure is for."

"I run a dog rescue foundation, Luis." She flexes her toes and sand trickles between them, catches on ridges of skin. "Why would I need companies in the British Virgin Islands? Or Barbados. Or New Zealand. Or Luxembourg. Or—"

"So you can take advantage of their treaties. They allow you to defer taxes indefinitely, and—"

"Listen to you." She chuckles, smooths the edge of the towel. "Treaties. Defer taxes. Five minutes with you and I feel like I need a tailored suit and a briefcase."

"And you hate boardrooms." Luis lowers his voice. "The fact remains, Pélagie, you're a woman of substantial wealth. It's my job to—"

"I don't want it." She turns those eyes on him, full blast. "Okay? That substantial wealth, as you call it, means nothing but—obligation. And damned if I'll skirt the obligations it comes with, too."

"I'm lost. What—?"

But she just keeps going. "The dogs balance it out. They make it—good. The money can do good, like this. See?"

There's a pleading in that last word that stops him from arguing. Of course he could keep arguing, even now that he doesn't understand what she's talking about—obligation? to whom?—because what good is a lawyer who can't debate three sides of an issue, can't push an advantage when he sees one. She could do so much more with the money that will otherwise go to the government in taxes. Save more dogs, if that's what she wants to do. But the conversation seems to have sidestepped into emotion he has no context for.

He should've let this go long ago. Ignored it back in April, like Milena wanted; processed the resignations last month, like Milena instructed. Milena was, as she always is, right. He's made this personal, but it isn't until now, when it's all about to end, that he realizes—admits—just how personal it's become.

And because it is personal, he has no choice. He must let it go. "We'll file the resignation documents tomorrow."

Pélagie glances at him. "Thank you."

"Don't thank me. The whole structure will fall apart."

But—and although this is not surprising, not anymore, it's still frustrating—she doesn't look worried. "Saves me the trouble of dissolving it."

"That's not how it works. Bank accounts will go inoperable pretty fast. They'll become inaccessible, even with your power of attorney. Might be a good idea to... Transfer assets. Before." He's just stating facts now. He hopes she understands that, if nothing else. Her disdain, for him and for the logic that rules his life, already crusts every exchange they have.

She's looking at her feet. "You're not supposed to be telling me any of this, I think."

"I can wait a day, to file. You'll have a busy day tomorrow, but you can get it done."

She looks up, she's going to say something, and hope blooms for Luis. An eleventh-hour reprieve—can it be? But he'll never know, because Al chooses that moment to come check up on his human. He barrels onto Luis, all drool and wet, sandy paws. All unreserved worship and joy, too, which is why Luis smiles instead of grimacing and doesn't even wipe away the gobs of saliva—it could be ocean water—on his arm. He does, however, apologize for the sand sprayed in Pélagie's direction. "He thinks he's a Chihuahua. Don't you, bud? Hey, are you thirsty, Al? Want some water?"

"I set a big bowl for them, too." Pélagie rubs the dog's chest, who looks for all the world like he's never experienced anything so luscious, the turncoat, as Luis pours from a thermos into the travel bowl.

Al splashes out double what he drinks, and is petted, patted, and scratched before running off to rejoin the other dogs—not without a vigorous shake devised to distribute equal amounts of water and sand on each human.

Luis sputters, spits sand. Pélagie laughs, wipes at her face with a hand that only smears more dog hair on her, finally peels off her tank top and declares, "I'm going to rinse off. It's the only way."

It takes Luis only a minute to take off shirt and shorts and follow her into the water, but in that minute memories of New Year's Eve crowd him—the walk on the beach with Milena, the fateful soak in the darkness, the drunken sex. Consequences. When he does wade in, he keeps a careful distance. Not that Pélagie would ever—hell, she doesn't even *like* him. He just doesn't want that dislike to become disdain.

He lets the moment, and the memories, dissolve in the gentle surge of the current. Then he says, in what might be a Guinness Record for Most Awkward Change of Subject: "You never told me how you got involved in dog rescuing."

"You mean how I became the crazy dog lady?" She grins, blows at the surface so the water ripples. "Don't apologize. Living with eighteen dogs qualifies me, I think. I'm even proud of it, which makes it so much more dysfunctional."

He laughs, and when she looks at him, the smoldering sunset lights her face like sun through stained glass.

"You really want to know?"

"I really do."

"It's a long story. And corny. Maudlin."

"I like maudlin." A lie, but it sounds convincing. Good lawyer, good boy. Or maybe it's not a lie. Because Luis is discovering he's fallen in love.

◆

I ora nos ta leu fo'i kas
Nos tur ta rekordá
Kòrsou su solo i playanan,
Orguyo di nos tur.

(And when we're far from home
We all remember
Curaçao's sun and beaches,
Pride of us all.)

~Fragment from Curaçao's
national anthem

July 2nd, Flag Day. People gather at Brionplein across
St. Annabaai from the postcard-perfect Handelskade.
Rectangles of blue with a yellow stripe fly from cars,
shops, homes, even office desks.
The blue is Pantone 280, the yellow Pantone 102.
In spite of their vibrancy, neither do justice to the ocean
and the sun they're meant to represent.

◆

Hot Water

July 1st

Luis Villalobos is using hot water in the shower for the first time since he moved to Curaçao. The tropical rock where opening a car window feels like holding a blow dryer to your face. Where cold showers are as coveted as they're impossible. Even at 2:00 am water won't get any cooler than lukewarm.

The mirror is still fogged up when he finishes dressing. Sweatpants, socks, the Timberland fleece he hasn't used since flying back from Mexico in May. His teeth won't stop chattering. And his head. Oh, his head.

Day Three of dengue fever. Who knew a mosquito could transmit such misery? He supposes he should be thankful it's not malaria. But dengue comes in varieties. According to Stepan, the closest thing to a friend Luis has here in Curaçao, one of these varieties makes you bleed to death, Ebola-like. Luis's brand-new doctor did say that's not the kind he has. But her assurances sounded perfunctory.

Luis doesn't handle illness well. Makes him feel vulnerable. Which he is, isn't everyone, and he understands this in the grooves of his subconscious the way he understands his forehand isn't as good as Nadal's and never will be. But in the heat of the game reality is malleable. Until it's Nadal on the other side of the net. Or, say, a deadly strain of dengue scorching your body.

He wants nothing more than to crawl back into bed. But Al has gone over twelve hours without a bathroom break.

And without food. He's waiting at the top of the stairs, doing his best to avoid fidgeting, imploring with big chocolate eyes.

Vulnerability.

"Let's go take a leak, bud."

Al tears down the two flights, nails skidding on wood then on granite tile. When Luis makes it all the way down, nausea blooming like an oil spill under his ribcage, Al is already at the patio doors, wiggling his vast body in spurts, as if impatience is vying with remorse for making such outrageous demands on his human.

"Sorry, bud. I should've let you out earlier. Thanks for—"

It takes him a whole new step to realize his foot is wet, another for the why to sink in, and then only because of the smell. "Oh, fuck."

Too late. He's already left a pee-soaked footmark on the rug.

Al cringes by the glass doors, massive shoulders scrunched down to the floor.

"Sshh, it's okay." Luis runs a hand over the dog's trembling head, the silky ears. One has a corner missing. Al came with many scars; most have healed, or disappeared under the regrowth of blue-black fur. Others, like this one, no amount of good food or kind hands can heal. "My fault, man. I know you tried."

As soon as the door unlatches, the dog dashes out onto the deck and around to his favorite palm. Luis leans against the door frame, shivering in the 32-Celsius breeze, and listens to the splash of Al's stream. Sounds like the freaking Nile.

Laughter startles him. No, it's not Al, having suddenly acquired a taste for either irony or the human means of expressing it. Besides, it came from the opposite corner of the deck. But the sound is familiar, pleasingly so. And unsettling. Doesn't belong here.

It belongs to Pélagie Solak.

Must be the fever. He should've stayed in bed, let Al turn the house into a Turkish-market toilet, the kind you roll up your pants to enter and throw away your shoes when you exit.

Al's on the deck, bladder urgencies either satisfied or forgotten, ears perked as high as they go. His face—his whole body—rigid. Listening.

The laughter comes again, from behind the feather hedge of palms separating his yard from Vikram's. Al streaks past him and leaps like a cheetah into the greenery.

"Al!"

But the dog has disappeared. Behind the palms, Vikram shouts something. Metal scrapes on wood. Then Pélagie's voice—it must be her, Al's hearing cannot lie: "Al? Hey, Al! Whatcha doing here?"

Pélagie here. Today. He's not only not at his best but at his worst of worsts. Life has a dirty-bastard sense of humor. At least the palms provide cover. She'll be spared the sight of him quivering like hummingbird wings, turned into this—this wuss. He pushes an arm through the mesh of greenness, far enough, he hopes, that it can be seen from the other side. "Hey, Vikram. Sorry about Al."

"Luis?" His neighbor sounds surprised, but not particularly angry. "Is it the weekend already?"

"No, man. I'm, uh, not feeling well." He catches intermittent glimpses through the palms, mostly of Vikram's pool, just large enough, like his, to escape jacuzzi status. No humans. No Al. "Al, come on, boy. He didn't hurt—uh, anyone, or make a mess, did he?"

"No, no, it's all—"

"We're fine."

It's Pélagie speaking, and her voice sends his flesh into a new eruption of shivers. "Okay. Good. And, uh, hi."

"Hi, Luis."

"How do you two know each other?" Vikram sounds

understandably bewildered.

"It's thanks to this guy," Pélagie says, and Luis imagines her scratching Al's chest, the pure pleasure on the dog's face. "Go on home, Al. Luis, call him."

"Here, boy. Al, come on. Let's go."

Nothing.

"I'll bring him around," Pélagie says.

Luis panics. There's dog pee in his fucking front hall. Will she smell it from the door? What if she wants to come in? But he has no energy to argue. All he seems able to do is call out a strong and virile, "Uh, okay."

The front bell rings as he climbs back up on the deck. How the hell did she go around so fast? He throws the rug over Al's puddle—the handwoven cotton is already stained, already doomed. Doorbell rings again. Keys, where are his keys? Kitchen counter? There, on the bookcase. "Coming. Hey, thanks for—"

But it's not Pélagie. It's Milena. His lover. His boss. She's wearing a filmy blouse of big sleeves and big neckline, heels so high and slim he wonders, as he often does, about the miracle of physics that keeps her upright.

"Luigi, I just heard. I would've flown back sooner if I'd known." She pushes past him, sophistication wafting in her wake, and heads down the hall towards the kitchen. "Did they do a blood test? Dengue is rare this time of year. God, you must be feeling like shit. What's that smell? And where's your monster mongrel? Listen, I had Zuleyda make you some chicken soup. She's such a good cook. I might take her to Singapore with me, just for the—Luis, close that door already."

But he doesn't. Pélagie's coming down the walk with Al. They both smile when they see Luis, but only Pélagie speaks. "So this is your secret lair, Mr. Hotshot Tax Attorney?"

Luis wants to lob back the banter, but his glibness has gone the way of the woolly mammoth. Emotion is building at the base of his throat, and he realizes that what he wants, more than his bed or the snugness of his duvet, more even than to feel well again, what he *needs*, actually, is this woman's arms around him. Which is mad, beyond unhinged, and not just because he's never felt those arms, has no idea how they'd feel, and how can he need something he's never had; no, all of that is true, and valid, but the reason it's certifiably insane to feel this way is because Pélagie isn't just out of his league: she's a different sport altogether.

He takes hold of Al's collar. "Thanks for bringing him back."

Pélagie squints at him. "You look—not well. Bad cold?"

"Dengue." There's a certain pride in not being vulnerable to just any common virus. He kind of wishes it was malaria now.

The square of skin between her eyebrows furrows. "How's the fever?"

"Under control." He shrugs.

She comes closer, lifts her hand. Before he can back away or say anything, she's touching his forehead. Cupping his cheek. Small and cool, that hand quiets the tomahawk army that's taken up residence in his skull. He leans into it, closes his eyes.

Milena is saying something from the kitchen. She probably found Al's puddle. She'll come looking for Luis, might be starting down the hall right fucking now, towards him, him and Pélagie and this suspended animation. And Milena has the instincts, the sensorial prodigy, of a lioness hunting. The question isn't *will she know:* it's *what will she do with the knowledge*. Luis's career is in her hands. He put it there, seven months ago to the fucking day.

Milena's footsteps are unmistakable now. Pélagie's hand moves, begins to slide from his cheek. A sort of disappointed relief blows through him. And then, just as the door begins to swing wider, just as Milena's perfume begins to claim the air, Luis crushes Pélagie to his chest—she's so lithe, so scrawny, and yet so vibrantly alive against him—and plants a lip-mashing, teeth-gnashing, make-the-dork-in-fifth-grade-proud kiss right on her mouth.

Al, with his usual disconnect from the complexities of human endeavor, barks in approval.

◆

Landhuis (n., Dutch, plural *landhuizen*)

Plantation or manor houses.
Original *landhuizen* in Curaçao date from as far back
as the 17th century, when the West Indies Company
distributed the island to settlers, though the *landhuis* style
is still used for modern constructions.

Landhuizen are famous today for the dash of color they give
the Curaçao landscape—yellow walls, red roofs, green
accents—but originally they were white.
Until 1817, when the Governor outlawed white buildings
due to the potentially damaging glare
they caused in the raw Curaçao sun—and,
legend has it, due to certain interests
he'd acquired in a paint manufacturing company.

◆

Quixote Always Loses
August 1st

The Curaçao branch of Ehrlich Fiduciary operates out of an eighteenth-century *landhuis* that's been declared a World Heritage site. As far as the property administrators are concerned, this alone justifies outrageous rent—which does not include maintenance; the tenant is responsible for the building's upkeep, and for carrying it out in accordance with very specific, very prohibitive, parameters. The sprawling plantation house is all high ceilings and French doors and wide verandas and hardwood shutters. The parquet floors, waxed every three months, make the clack of Milena Durant's favorite Jimmy Choos echo through the halls. When she's working late she goes barefoot, which has made her privy to much she shouldn't be. Information is mighty currency.

But the grapevine isn't infallible.

The best view in the building, hands down, is from the south side of Wing B. From Milena's office, to be exact. Caribbean blue in sky and sea fills three quarters of the window behind her desk. The riot-colored buildings of the Handelskade—that cupcake Amsterdam, the unofficial icon of this tiny and otherwise unknown island—fill the remaining quarter. A bright cruise ship, Royal Caribbean judging by the size, perches today like overripe fruit in the middle ground.

The view is wasted on the two people in Milena's office. She's paging, somewhat vaguely, through a yellow legal pad. The man sitting across the desk from her, Ehrlich worldwide CEO Rowan Barry, has turned his chair sideways, and seems deep in contemplation of the shirt buttons straining over the zeppelin of his belly.

"Is this going to be a problem?"

Milena looks up, but he's still gazing at his stomach. A touch of mutiny creeps into her reply. "Why would it?"

He sucks on his lower lip. "You and I don't often clash on judgment issues. I thought you might be... disappointed."

"Disappointment implies gain was expected. I've nothing to gain from who takes my place. Surprised, yes. Not disappointed."

"He was your hire. You did expect—"

"He was *your* hire, Rowan. Remember? I wanted to hire that ballbreaker from London to replace Stepan as Legal Counsel and make *Stepan* Managing Director. You were the one who insisted on Luis."

"He's Latin. The Latin American market is going to hell. Especially the Mexican market. Someone like him, with his connections, his track record, can make all the difference."

"Which explains why I'm surprised."

Rowan taps his thumbs on the tautness of his stomach, a pensive drumroll. "He'll be a great MD. One day. When he's not so raw. So full of—" He tilts back the granite block of his head, looks for the word he wants—which, apparently, isn't *shit*—in the ceiling beams. "Idealism. Pipe dreams. You know what I mean. You were, too, at one point."

"So were you. All of us."

He looks at her. "An MD can't be a Quixote."

"He'll grow out of it. We all—"

"I have ample faith he will. What I'm saying—what the Board is saying—is not *yet*. You need to name your

74

successor. You need to begin the transition. Stepan is chomping at the bit to get started."

Milena leans back, and her chair creaks a complaint. "Stepan knows? You spoke to him already?"

"We had to know if he was on board." Rowan's lids droop to half-mast.

Why did she think there was still a chance, that her window—Luis's window—was still open? "He'll leave, you know."

Rowan uses the corner of a post-it pad to clean under the nail of his thumb. "He's bluffing."

"It's the only reason he came here. To be MD. He'll have nothing to stay for." And he'll blame her. He'll think it's because of that stupid fight. Her tantrum over that woman. He'll think she's punishing him. Which wouldn't be so farfetched if it was anyone else.

Her mother defined love as wishing for someone else's happiness more than you wish for your own. Over the last month, Milena has had to come to terms with the fact she might be—no, is—in love. The worst kind.

The kind without a future. (She's leaving, Luis is staying.)

The unrequited kind. (She's no naïf.)

The kind where none of the above makes a whit of difference.

And the only thing she has to give that might be of any value at all to him—her current job—isn't, it's been decided, hers to give after all.

Rowan rests an elbow on the desk. "Luis wants to leave, let him. But I'll bet you next year's NOPAT he won't. I'll bet you this year's *and* next year's."

"What if he does, Rowan?"

"He's too proud. How would he explain leaving Cabrera y Machado in Mexico City for this nine-month stint in the Caribbean? He won't be happy, sure, but he'll finish his contract."

"And if you're wrong? Are we willing to lose him?"

He studies her with those half-lidded eyes. Frog eyes. Cold eyes. "Are you? How far would you go to avoid losing him? If this were your call, would you hand over this office—*your* office—to Luis? Now?"

Luis, who still cares so much about Doing The Right Thing. Luis, who refuses to grasp the basic give-and-take that keeps this business running. Luis, who has no guile in his soul—not even enough to realize how transparent his Man Of The World act is. Luis, who expects that world to function according to karmic rules or something. Being completely objective, all emotion aside, all personal involvement—even if objectivity isn't something she feels capable of right now—there can only be one answer.

"No," she says, and guilt feels like the Devil whispering in her ear.

"Good." Rowan stands, stretches. Nonchalant. Heedless of the lives lying in shards around him. "Look into that replacement for Stepan, will you? The—what did you call her? The ballbreaker?"

"She's with Ernst & Young now. Legal for LatAm. We'd have to offer her diamonds and pearls to get her here."

"Would she consider MD in a couple of years? Stepan wants to go to Luxembourg. You know he turned down Singapore? Said he's had it with tropical weather."

Her stomach turns a triple axel, lands wrong, doesn't quite recover. "What about Luis?"

Rowan shrugs. "A little competition won't hurt him. Might even help him."

Luis will hate—no, revile her. But that won't be as bad as knowing the damage she's inflicted on his career. Because her fucking him did, in fact, fuck him over. If she hadn't been sleeping with him, she'd have made damn sure he was ready. Instead, she coddled him. Didn't push hard enough.

Didn't coach him the way she should have. Not in the office, anyway.

Perhaps she can still help him. Not that he'll ever know, or believe it if he did. "I agree, Rowan, that Luis isn't ready now. But he'll be a kick-ass MD one day, not too far in the future. Ehrlich would do well to make sure he doesn't leave us before then."

Rowan acknowledges that with a single nod. "Sounds good. But at what price?"

"Forget about that London woman. It wouldn't work out, and even if it did, she'd be ridiculously expensive. Wasn't the Brazil Legal Counsel looking to relocate? He knows Stepan, they've worked together already. They'd make a good team." And with his Compliance background, Milena thinks, he's unlikely to have MD ambitions. He won't be a rival for Luis.

"It's an option."

"A good option. It'll make it easier to convince Luis of staying."

Rowan nods again, noncommittally, and turns to go. That's it, that's all the assurance she'll get. Now she has to find the way—and the balls—to break it to Luis.

With a hand on the door, Rowan turns back. "What about Singapore?"

"What about it?"

"Latin American countries, especially Mexico, have interesting treaty structures with Singapore. Lots of opportunities for someone with the kind of know-how he has. Something to consider, perhaps."

Milena feels cold creeping up to her face. "You mean— Luis should go in my stead?"

Rowan chuckles, dry as winter-chapped lips. "I don't want him running a branch but you think I'd give him a position on the Board? Come on, Milena. I meant an—I don't know, a directorship maybe, something like that. Get him to run a few projects, get him involved with sales maybe. Or he could work with Asian clients. A new challenge for him."

"He was in Hong Kong for two years with HSBC." Her head is spinning.

"Even better. Given free rein he might come up with some innovative structuring for Asian investments in LatAm. Make us all wildly rich and powerful." He winks at her, opens the door. "I'm sure you could rustle up something interesting for him there. If you wanted to."

Rowan, the bastard, always manages to find that most secret hope: one's most contemptible temptation. And then he holds it out, a careless child squeezing a baby chick, daring you to do something, anything, before he squashes it to death.

◆

No place quite like Bonaire to relax and recharge.
Do the math: one hundred square miles, sixteen thousand
inhabitants. (Not counting flamingos. Or donkeys.)
Sailing enthusiasts, windsurfers, kite surfers, and scuba
divers abound—the entire reef system surrounding
the island is a protected marine park; it's like swimming
in an aquarium. The water is so clear that dive lights
aren't necessary on night dives, even with a waning moon.
There's no traffic, no traffic lights; there's good food, to
cater to the educated palates of such diverse
and international visitors.

In the Caribbean, Shangri-La goes by *Bonaire*.

◆

The Bonaire Feel-Good
September 1st

There's a new bounce in Luis Villalobos's step this Monday morning. He takes the sweeping stairs to the Ehrlich Fiduciary building two by two and dances a Rocky Balboa victory hop at the summit, face lifted up to the morning sun. The wind in his ears could be the roar of an adoring crowd.

The receptionist pushes one half of the glass doors open for him. Was she watching? Well, what if she was? He gives her a big smile. "Bon día, Rochandra." He's making an effort with Papiamentu, now that he has a private tutor. Of sorts.

Rochandra looks him up and down. "Bon dia i bon siman."

Bon siman. He always forgets that on Mondays. Not just *good morning* but also *good week*. What a lovely custom. He's never seen it anywhere else; maybe it's unique to Curaçao.

Curaçao. He came so close to leaving without giving this island a chance. He'd have missed so much. Al, for instance. And Pélagie.

"There's a package for you." Rochandra brandishes a clipboard. "You want to sign for it now, or shall I send the messenger up later?"

"Now's fine. Danki."

She hauls a FedEx box onto the counter and hands him the clipboard. "Had a good weekend?"

He scans the spreadsheet of incoming correspondence for his name. "More than good, actually."

Rochandra is leaning on the counter, the picture of an eager high school gossip—notwithstanding the gray hair and the fact she weighs roughly four times what the average teenager would. "Did you do something special? Maybe meet someone special?"

"No. Well, yes. I guess. I, uh… I went to Bonaire."

"Bonaire?" Maybe it's the way he hesitated, or the way his gaze slid away from hers, but Rochandra is looking like a hyena that's just spotted a wounded gazelle all alone in the savannah. "I never pegged you for a lover of peace and quiet. Why would you go to Bonaire?"

"Well, I—"

"Oh, you're a diver! I forgot, yes. And? You loved it, no?"

"Yes, it's—"

"But your dog must've missed you. Poor thing, left all alone."

Normally, Luis finds Curaçao's corporate informality refreshing. Right now, though, he's missing the distance that deference provides. It's unsettling that a receptionist should know so much about his life. "He went with me. Sorry, I can't find where I'm supposed to sign."

He pushes the clipboard back to her, but she doesn't even notice. She's staring at him, quite literally agape. "You took your *dog* to Bonaire?"

He forces a smile. "Rochandra. Where do I need to sign?"

She lifts an eyebrow, miffed but not chastised, and flips with exaggerated gestures to another page. "Right *here*. Where your *name* is."

When he's Managing Director—the announcement should be made any day now—he'll hire a new receptionist.

As he hands back the clipboard, something catches his eye. "Is this date right? This FedEx box came in on Thursday?"

She barely glances at the page. "If that's what the manifest says."

The package most likely contains incorporation documents—which might have generated immediately collectible revenue if delivered last week. No point in belaboring the issue; not today, not with this attitude. He thanks her again, doesn't get a reply.

His Bonaire feel-good is fading fast.

He'll bring up the mailroom at the Efficiency Development Team meeting. He rescheduled it for today; he and Al had to meet Pélagie at the airport at three on Friday, so he took the afternoon off. First time he's done that since he arrived in Curaçao back in December. But with US banks closed today—it's Labor Day—he'll have plenty of time to catch up.

His phone rings as he walks to the elevator. Fifty bucks—fifty thousand—say it's Milena again. He expected a big scene—who wouldn't, after her soap opera back in July—so he put off telling her about this burgeoning thing with Pélagie longer than he should have, but she's been surprisingly mature about it. Until Saturday, when she apparently lost it. Forty-three missed calls over the weekend. This morning, when the plane landed and Pélagie handed back the Blackberry she'd confiscated on Friday (that was the deal: no expectations, no cheesiness, no Ehrlich. *The financial world does revolve without you* were, he thought, her exact words), the device had buzzed and pinged and chimed and vibrated itself half to battery death. Voice mail, texts, even emails asking, pleading, then finally demanding he call Milena.

For an adrenaline-soaked moment there at the airport, Luis panicked. Had something happened? Some emergency? A client dead, his heirs clamoring for the big bucks their dad or grandpa thought he'd so smartly hidden away? A subpoena from the IRS—or, worse, from Interpol? It's happened. But there are procedures in place to deal with that and more. No, knowing Milena, it's either plain jealousy—somehow she found out he was with Pélagie and maturity abandoned her—or, more likely, it's some bullshit about the MD announcement. She's theatrical, wants it to come off all Cirque de Soleil. Useless, and moot; everyone already knows the job is his. But she's still MD now. He'll drop off his things in his office and go find her, find out what killer bee got into her designer bonnet, and tell her, nicely, to calm the fuck down.

The elevator arrives with a muted ding. As the doors open, he hears Rochandra's internal line buzzing and her voice, sans the mood, when she answers. "Bon dia, dushi. Oh, he just—he's going up now. No, no, he's already in the elevator."

It's got to be Milena. Luis calls out, "Someone looking for me?"

He hears the clack of the receiver being returned to its cradle before she replies. "No. No one."

Could he have misunderstood? No; there's no one else here. This is bordering on insubordination. Anywhere else in the world he'd call her on it, but Curaçao has quirky labor laws. He's watched Milena jump through hoops of fire to avoid employment litigation. Best to take it up with HR first.

Goodbye, Bonaire feel-good.

But he'll be back. Pélagie goes at least once a month to check on the shelter there. He's pretty sure he earned a standing invitation after his performance this weekend. He catches his own eye in the elevator mirror. *Tiger.*

No, it's not the sex. It was good, *he* was good, which doesn't always happen when he's that into someone; he seems to do best on casual between-the-sheets encounters. Less pressure, maybe. Lower stakes. Not that this—this *thing* with Pélagie is going anywhere. She's been very clear, if not very vocal: she has no inclination for romantic entanglements. He senses an old hurt there; he's an idiot for not leaving it alone. But she says it's all about the now. You, me, here, why not. She's big on the fact of coincidence, not its significance.

The self-serving ego-trip junkie in him insists she's right.

He committed to the MD job here for two years; spending even just a fraction of that time with Pélagie will make it not just bearable but memorable. And after that... Well. She knows he's leaving. It's not like he's lied, or made any kind of *promises*—

The elevator doors slide open to Wendolyn's smile. A frantic sort of smile.

"Morning. Not good, by the looks of you. What's wrong?"

"Wrong? Nothing!" Her voice is pitched higher than usual, and her grip, as she takes hold of his arm, feels jittery. "But there's, uh, something I need you to look at. It's on my desk."

"I'll be right there. Let me leave this in my—"

"Do that after. Super urgent, uh, loan agreement. The bank's waiting."

She's tugging on his arm, which had a better chance of working without the backdrop of Rochandra's cheekiness. "They can wait ten seconds more," he says.

"Please! It's—"

That's when he hears the shouting. It's Milena, and it's coming from the direction of his office. The direction Wendolyn seems bent on keeping him away from. The grip of her hand is so tight his shirt is wrinkling. "Wendolyn? What's going on?"

She says something, but he's already moving past her towards the sound of Milena in full-blown rage.

"I don't care if the email came from GOD HIMSELF! Take this shit down *now*! How dare you, how FUCKING—"

Luis strides around the corner and the scene freezes into a diorama. Josinelle, Stepan's elderly assistant, cowering just inside the door to Stepan's office and clutching, incongruously, a bouquet of red balloons. Behind her, even more incongruously, Stepan himself, standing on his own desk and holding the dangling half of a CONGRATS! banner. The other half is still taped to the top of the window frame. More red balloons, tied together in bouquets of three, litter the floor under him. The new legal intern, whose name Luis can't remember—has he even met her? she looks completely unfamiliar, but then so does everything else right now—stands by the whiteboard on the opposite wall. Someone spent a valuable chunk of time drawing a two-tone poster on it, which the intern is—was—erasing. Only the lower right corner remains; a too-large exclamation mark surrounded by childishly cute stars and pointillist umbrellas that Luis assumes represent fireworks. It must've been drawn a day ago, at least, because the ghost of the foot-high letters the girl has just erased is still all too visible.

Congrats, new MD!
You deserve it!

Milena stares at him from the doorway, fury melting like butter on a griddle. "Why the bloody fuck didn't you return my calls?"

◆

The flag of Curaçao has two five-pointed stars: a large one for Curaçao itself and a smaller one for Klein Curaçao, the divers' paradise just off the main island's eastern tip. The five points represent the five continents Curaçao's inhabitants come from. This tiny speck of land, population 150,000, is home to fifty nationalities. *Fifty*.

◆

Illusions, Lethal Weapons, and a Can of Maggots

October 1st

The sunlight, already sharp this early, makes the skin of Pélagie's back glow like honey lit from below. Luis has only minutes before she wakes. She's up every morning at six, no alarm. In a different time zone, would she wake up at six Curaçao time? Or does her body tune into the ebb and flow of day, like a radio? Maybe he'll find out if she comes to visit him in London.

She won't, though. What they have, beautiful—surprisingly, arrestingly exquisite—as it is, is also inherently momentary. (And isn't that what adds the edge?) He experiences childish relief every time she agrees to see him. Every kiss, every orgasm, every time he makes her smile; it's all just another turn in the unwinding of their clock.

He settles back on the pillow, sideways so that Pélagie's skin fills his view. He doesn't have to spell out the thought to feel the bite of regret: he's going to miss her. Another in the long list of reasons to despise Milena.

"Please don't stare at me." Pélagie's voice, rough with morning gravel, startles him.

"I'm not."

"Is that your hallmark? Staring your lovers awake?" Her foot finds his leg under the bedsheets, but he's faster now; before her toes find purchase, he swings both legs out into the air-conditioned chill and onto the covers.

Even through the Swiss duvet—which he's been carrying around since his time in Zurich, like some sort of security blanket—he feels a pinch on his calf hard enough he's sure it left a bruise. "Ow!"

"I barely touched you."

"Your feet should be registered as lethal weapons."

He rolls on top of her, pushes his weight into her, and for an instant he's giddy with the illusion of dominance. That's all it is, though. A charade. How can someone so tiny—he can encircle both her wrists with one hand, her feet look like a doll's when she shuffles around in his flip-flops, his shirts reach more than halfway down her thighs—be so strong?

Maybe it's not about strength, but about weakness. His, in fact. Take the sex: he's always watching himself, measuring out passion like a nineteenth-century chemist preparing laudanum tincture. Detachment is power to some; Luis knows better. Confidence breeds fearless love, fearless sex. He's no monument to poise, sexual or otherwise, but he's never been this self-conscious. It's not the slightness of her body; Pélagie has proven, in and out of bed, to be anything but fragile. The risks of emotional investment feel closer to the mark, but that's stupid. He'll be gone before either of them get a chance to invest anything in anyone.

She lifts her head up from the pillow, reaching for a kiss. He pulls away. "I haven't brushed my teeth yet."

"Eww, morning breath." She grins, and the sunshine glows brighter. "Kiss me anyway."

Instead, he blurts it out. "Will you come visit me in London?"

"You're taking the job?" Her smile broadens. Should she be so happy he's leaving? No attachments, yes, but isn't unbridled joy at his departure carrying it a bit far?

And yet, whether for pride or masochism, or a quaint, uniquely masculine, mix of both, he can't stop himself. To avoid that bright smile while he rips the lid off this can of

90

maggots, he bends to nuzzle her neck. "I'm thinking about it. If you'll visit. Will you?"

There's a heave from under him and then he's on his back and Pélagie is pinning *him* down. "Who cares if I visit? You said London was, I quote, the best opportunity to get your career back on track." She bites his chin. "End quote."

He grasps her wrists; so slight, like twigs that might snap with one wrong move. Sometimes he wishes she were—no, not fatter, just... heftier. More substance. Like that adage for legal documents, *substance over form*; he loves her body, the grace in the very lack of substance, but the practical aspect of interacting with such a body makes him feel like the proverbial bull in a museum of rare Ming porcelain. "I care."

"Well, don't." The lightness of her kiss does nothing to soften the admonition. She bounds off the bed, away from him and his grip with nary an effort. "Can I take a quick shower?"

"Go ahead," he says. A shower together isn't on the table. She emphasized *quick*. And there's her refusal to talk visits.

Al is waiting downstairs. Loyal, unconditional Al, who rushes out to his favorite palm tree every morning, no matter how early, to let out a stream of decades-long pent-up pee.

He's going to miss the dog, too.

When Pélagie joins them, wet hair smelling of his shampoo—and what pleasure he derives from these small, small things—he's out on the porch with two mugs of coffee.

"I don't have time," she says, but she picks up a mug anyway. "Got to be at the vet at—damn, now. It's going to be a hell of a day. Six dogs scheduled for sterilization."

He sips at his coffee. "Plans for tonight?"

"Home, with the convalescing. Why?" Her fingernail clicks out got-to-get-going in Morse code on the coffee mug. Or maybe it's don't-get-all-clingy-on-me.

"There's something I want to ask. It's about Al," he adds, as incentive.

"The traveling stuff? You know I'm more than happy to help with—"

"I can't take him with me. London is—I'll be in a tiny apartment, working sixteen hours a day. It's no life for him. And the weather. He's used to the warmth, the sun…"

Pélagie's face is blank. If he tapped it with a knuckle, it would most likely sound hollow and dry. Like a wooden mask. And her voice is flatter than the surface of a mirror when she says, "You're going to leave your dog behind."

"I have no choice. And it's the best thing for him. He'd—"

"Please. It's the best thing for *you*. Dogs are forever animals, Luis. They don't understand human circumstances changing. To him, this is abandonment. You rescued him from the street; surely you can see how horrible it is for him to go back to—"

"I'm not sending him back to the street!" Anger sparks to life at the base of his throat. He sits back, crosses a leg, breathes in. "That's why I'm asking—I wanted to ask—if you would take him in. He knows you already. *I* know you. He couldn't be in better hands."

Pélagie's mug cracks down on the patio table. "I, personally, already own sixteen dogs. As an organization, we have over a hundred and forty dogs looking for a home. We never have enough space, enough foster homes, enough volunteers, enough anything. Least of all time. How is coming to me better for Al than having his own human?"

"But I can't take him! I'd make other arrangements, Pélagie, if I had time, but—I mean, how was I supposed to know I'd be leaving so soon?"

"You did, though. You knew you were here for only a year or two. Sooner or later, you would've left. And still you took him in."

Luis leans forward. Why is she making this so difficult? "He needed a home, he—"

"And now he doesn't? You—" She turns her head away, takes a breath. "I love what I do, you know that. You also know how violently I hate that it's necessary. A perfect world, for me, would be a place where all of us animal rescuers were out of a job. But we're decades—centuries—away from that. Because of people like you. Damn you, Luis. I thought you were different."

He's shocked into silence. Not so much by the insult—he sees her point, of course he does, but his situation is different. She'd understand if she weren't so biased. So goddamn stubborn. No, his shock comes from having seen, just before she disappeared into the house, a glistening at the corner of her eye.

He is suspicious of women's tears. They may not be always manipulatively produced, but they always manipulate *him*. He didn't think Pélagie was like that.

I thought you were different, she'd said.

I thought you were different, too.

"I'll take Al." She's standing by the porch doors, dry-eyed, face again a mask.

"Thank you. I know it's—"

"I'll come get him over the weekend. I'll email you."

"Hey, no rush. I'm still here for another month. I'd like—"

"The sooner he begins to adapt to your absence, the better. For him. And it's all about what's best for the dog, right?"

"Come on, Pélagie—"

93

"Don't. Aside from whatever arrangements we need to discuss for Al, I'd really prefer to avoid all contact."

Al watches her leave from the edge of the porch. Inscrutable.

"Come here, boy."

The dog comes to Luis without hesitation, always eager, always trusting. *You have no clue what's about to happen, do you?* Luis strokes the silky ears.

Al gazes up at him, panting. Is he maybe a bit too close? A tad less relaxed? Is Luis just imagining what he wants to see?

Pélagie says dogs can smell anything. Emotions: fear, anxiety, anger. Intentions. Lies. *What does goodbye smell like, Al?*

◆

Diversity is as much a part of the Curaçao soul as the wind and the heat. People have come and gone—invaded, occupied, brought by force or by choice—for as long as humans have lived on this rock. Before the 20th century even began, Curaçao was already a melting pot of culture and heritage, and a gateway between Latin America and Europe. Then came the trust industry, and more foreigners, from further afar. Which makes for a fascinating social life—and one serious drawback: many of these imports are only temporary. As common as farewell parties are, goodbyes never seem to get any easier.

◆

The Inevitable
November 1st

There's something biblical about downpours in Curaçao. Rain crashes down in windblown sheets that whip water in directions that defy gravity, into puddles that become ponds, that become white-crested lagoons.

Luis's porch—ex-porch, now—is slick with water. The sliding doors are beaded with splash, even under the porch roof. The saline lake down below, the cacti-and-scraggly-bush landscape that greeted him every morning, now sports fringes of vibrant green.

It won't last, Luis knows. As soon as the rain season is over—January, maybe February if the island's lucky—the sun will bake the green back into withered brown. He saw it happen during his first months here. And now he's leaving before it happens again.

The click of a lock disengaging, and the front door opens with its usual dragging catch on the front step. So easy to fix: he would've done it himself if he'd had a sander.

Marjan walks into the hall shaking out her hair, leaving wet footprints. Luis has no right to be annoyed. He's here only to turn in his keys, after all. She and Vikram, his neighbors—ex-neighbors—have taken on the administration of the condos. "Sorry I'm late. Vikram had a flat on the Emancipatie Boulevard, and you know how bad that floods." She barks laughter, and Luis thinks of Al. Not that he needs special prompts for that. The dog's absence has emptied Luis's life.

"It's all right. I just got here myself."

Marjan keeps up a steady commentary: about the weather, the island government fiascos, the injustice of Vikram being unable to take vacation in December. ("People with kids get priority," she says. "That's discrimination, isn't it? So unfair, really.") She follows him upstairs into the master bedroom and bath, guest bedroom and bath, back downstairs to the laundry room, living room, kitchen. His cleaning lady did a good job. Great, in fact. When Marjan opens the refrigerator, Luis gets a whiff of chilled lemon-scent Disiclin.

"Looks like you did my job for me." Marjan looks around, nods, presumably happy. "The new tenant could move in today."

"It's been rented? Already?" He didn't expect this twinge of loss.

"You kidding? These condos go like fresh stroopwafels at the Haarlem market. Especially towards the end of the year. All you corporate guys move at the same time, apparently."

He doesn't know what to say. His stuff is packed; two suitcases in the hotel room he'll call home until his flight on Tuesday, three boxes at the movers' warehouse. The house he lived in for eleven months has been washed and cleaned of him, his presence, his life. Why, then, does it still feel so *his?*

But Marjan isn't waiting for a reply. "Must be so exciting. Every few years a new country, new people, new weather..." She looks up from the documents she's paging through on the polished concrete of the kitchen counter. "Though—London you said, eh? You could've waited for spring."

No, he couldn't, even though Srikantha, his old college buddy and now his new boss, told him—the kind of for-your-college-buddy's-ears-only thing he probably regretted as soon as he said it—that Management was so elated at landing someone with Luis's track record they'd wait as long as it took. But Luis was eager, too. Everything about Curaçao screamed his failures back at him, steel claws on a blackboard everywhere he looked, everything he did. Every memory he had.

Marjan scrawls out an IOU for the security deposit. He'll drop it off at the office on his way back to the hotel. He turned in his keycard yesterday, before his farewell happy hour, but Saturdays are busy at Ehrlich Curaçao. Someone will let him in.

Or maybe he'll just slip it into the mailbox. Avoid a second round of goodbyes. And potentially running into Milena.

At the front door he hands over his keys, free of the HSBC keyring that has graced the open-sesame to his homes for the last six years. There's a finality in this handing over, and he would've liked to linger in the moment, mark it somehow, but Marjan snatches them up without ceremony and the moment is gone. "So..." she says, in that unique, drawn-out way the Dutch have, which always reminds Luis of Maria teaching the von Trapp children the notes on an Austrian mountaintop. "Enjoy your trip, and much success in London." She gives him the three standard Dutch pecks on the cheeks—*three, because they're free*—and pats his shoulder in an awkward pseudo-hug.

"Thank you. For—well, for all your help."

"Graag gedaan. Doei!" She waves and disappears back into the house. The front door catches with a muffled scrape before slamming closed.

He should've borrowed a sander.

His black Wrangler Rubicon Jeep is, of course, gone. It lasted three whole days after Al left with Pélagie. He drove it to the carwash, told the guys he'd give them each fifty guilders if they got every last dog hair out, and when they were done he drove it straight to the dealer's second-hand lot. He has a rental now, a white automatic Kia sedan that smells of too many people and cheap something-berry deodorizer, that feels too low on the road, that lacks the Jeep's grace in everything from windshield wiper action to the silky suede of its upholstery.

Which is, in fact, the point.

And yet, even a car without memories is capable of reading a driver's mind. Luis doesn't remember making a right instead of a left on the Caracasbaaiweg; he doesn't remember any of the other turns he must have made to get away from the shops and traffic lights and into the wild, thorny clusters of the *mondi*. He doesn't remember any conscious thought, in fact, until the tires bump down onto rutted dirt and his right foot, working on instinct, steps off the accelerator to work the brake. When his left foot pumps air instead of a clutch pedal, when his right hand grabs for the Jeep's sleek gearshift and finds instead the clammy plastic of the Kia's handbrake—that's when he returns from wherever he was and looks up in time to see the sign before the car passes under it: Sint Joris Baai.

The dog beach.

Fuck.

This is a bad idea. Even if Pélagie hadn't forbidden all contact, not just with her but—especially—with Al. Even if Luis didn't wholeheartedly agree that a clean break was the only way to go, the only way to help Al—Luis himself—move forward. On the other hand, it's freakin' *raining*. More of a drizzle now, but still. Pélagie wouldn't bring her dogs, any dog, out in this weather. Al is safe, dry, on a pile of blankets, in an extra-large basket, somewhere in a corner of Pélagie's house. This is the absolute last place Al would be found today.

All right, then. A private moment of nostalgia. One for the road.

He drives on, gut feeling like a misshapen cat's cradle, until the road widens, the gray-green of the bay fills the windshield, the tires crunch more sand than dirt—and he sees the impossible: Pélagie's red Explorer, muddy as always, parked by the makeshift benches.

No sign of her, though. Or of dogs. Luis can turn around and leave without ever being seen. Drive back to town, to the Ehrlich building, to his hotel; brush up on UK statutes and treaties, keep marking time in the limbo his life has become, until Tuesday and the airport and the plane and leaving all this—failure, heartbreak, disappointment—behind. Start over. Sluice that slate down.

He parks alongside the Explorer. He was right: it's empty.

The air smells raw, like just-picked mushrooms. The wind barely amounts to a breeze; he steps out, braced for the Kia's door to be ripped out of his grasp as usual, but it just teeters on its hinges. He has to actually push it closed. In the stillness, the fading rain polka-dots his shirt and kisses his face, his arms. It makes the flat surface of the bay whisper; a *sshhh* that feels more like commiseration than admonition.

There they are. In a replay of the scene from April—exactly, he realizes with a sensation of fateful intervention, seven months ago—Pélagie is walking along the curve of the bay. She might even be wearing the same clothes: the dark yoga pants, the loose green tank top. This time, though, there's only one dog with her. The only dog possible.

Al lopes quietly, leashless, by Pélagie's side. He was always far ahead of Luis, running back and forth: faster, Human, faster! Sniffing here and there and oh, over there! Now the dog's head hangs steady, incurious, except when he looks up at Pélagie every few steps. For guidance? Or is he making sure she's still there?

The landscape blurs; it's the wind, dust in his eyes. He swipes at them. Drive away, dammit. Before—

Too late. Al's head comes up, sniffing, looking this way. Then—just like April, but in the opposite direction—the dog is off, sprinting like a cheetah, wet sand lifting in tufts behind him. Pélagie whistles—at least Luis assumes it's her, because his eyes are glued to the black giant barreling toward him—but the dog doesn't slow. Then the dunes cut off Luis's view. In seven seconds Al will be over the top, three more and he'll be all over Luis.

Get in the car.

Luis leans against the Kia, bracing himself. For the weight of Al's wet, sandy body. For the wrath he'll incur from Pélagie. For the consequences. For the inevitable.

◆

Water in Curaçao—extracted from the ocean and
desalinized—is expensive to the point of luxury. The bright
side: Evian straight out of the tap (the desalinization
process, reverse electrolysis, is also purifying).
The down side: landscaping requires a serious,
long-term investment.

Local lore has it that Curaçao soil, when it comes to
growing things, is worthless. Beware of lore, local or not.
The problem isn't the soil; it's the fresh water supply. As of
2015, Curaçao is producing wine, and sustainable-living
farms have cropped up, too (pun intended). How? Wells.
Fresh water is plentiful under the bedrock, and modern
surveying and drilling technology have made it accessible.

◆

The Miracle of Small Things
December 1st

Monday nights are always crowded at De Heeren. Not a single empty table inside, not even on the patio. Familiar faces turn my way, hands raise, fingers wiggle hello. I see a few nudges; more faces turn, even from tables full of strangers. *Look, it's Curaçao's crazy dog lady.* Too late for regrets. Not many places to pick from on a Monday, anyway.

The hostess gives me a bright smile. "Goeden avond," she says. "Inside or outside, Ms. Solak?"

Inside there's more light. Inside, the hum of conversation will cover awkward silences. Which begs the question: why should I care? "Outside," I say. Dagger of awkwardness, find thy sheath.

"Just five minutes while we set it up."

I wander over to the bar and make small talk with some of those familiar faces, people whose names I make no effort to remember, people who might, or might not, believe they're my friends. I ignore the veiled once-overs the glitzy women give my jeans and my flip-flops until the hostess taps my arm. "Your table is ready."

Dekko, the manager, is waiting outside, full of apologies. The table barely catches the edge of the patio lighting. In the darkness, its candle centerpiece hollers *romantic.* "I have better spots, but only inside," he says.

And then I see him, striding into the restaurant with those long legs. His hair is longer, his shirt is untucked, the sleeves rolled up, but it looks freshly ironed. His feet, though, are the key: the great Luis Villalobos is wearing flip-flops—*flip-flops!*—to a restaurant.

"It's okay, Dek. This is fine."

He says something about sending over a bottle of wine and I nod and say thanks (I think). Luis is scanning faces in the half-light. When he sees me, he grins, and it's that same arrogant hot-shot attitude. The flip-flops are only a prop; he hasn't changed.

After a dicey moment of greeting—he goes for the kiss on the cheek, which I should've expected, him being Mexican and all, but it still feels invasive—he sits down across from me. "I wasn't sure you'd come," he says.

I give him what I hope looks like a non-committal smile. "How are you?"

"Good. You?"

He looks happy. More relaxed even than in Bonaire that one luscious weekend. Maybe it's the tan, the weight he's lost. All that lugging around of tanks in the sun. "Enjoying your new career?"

He nods, looks down at the table. "So far, yeah."

"Being a dive instructor was a lifelong ambition?"

He laughs. "I'm not an instructor. And no, not remotely. But I do love it."

"So far." A gibe. I can't help myself.

He lets out his breath with a *whoosh*. "So far."

Where the hell is Dekko and the wine? A waiter at least, maybe some water? "How's Al?"

"Great." He smiles that tender, childish smile of his, the one that gave me faith in humanity. "Our neighbor has a Rottweiler puppy—well, not a real one, a mix, but he looks Rottweiler-ish—and he and Al totally hit it off."

"I'm glad he has company while you're working."

"Actually, he comes to work with me."

I want to frown, to show I disapprove—Al isn't exactly the world's most socialized dog, and Luis isn't going to win any behavior specialist awards any time soon—but the sheer absurdity of the image trumps everything and makes me chuckle. "You bring Al with you to work?"

He laughs. "Pretty awesome for the guy who didn't even like dogs, right?"

Pretty glib for the guy who was going to leave his dog behind is what I think. But I don't say it. Anger is nothing but hurt; revealing it makes us vulnerable. And I'm done being vulnerable. "Where are you living?"

"Montaña. Tiny house, but a huge yard. All walled in. At night the stars are amazing. And rent's affordable on my new salary."

Montaña? How far the great have fallen. "Is it safe, though?"

He chuckles. "I'm from Mexico City, remember? This island is the safest place on Earth."

"Don't get cocky, Luis. It's the—"

Dekko arrives with two bottles. "I have an Argentinian merlot and a Spanish tempranillo, both excellent. If you're having meat, I'd suggest—"

"We're not eating," I say. "The merlot—"

"The tempranillo sounds good." Luis puts a hand on mine. An apology for interrupting, or is he marking territory for Dek's benefit—or mine?

"Bit heavy, no?" I slide my hand away, disguise the movement by rummaging in my bag for my phone.

"This one's very light," Dek says, and for once I resent his solicitude. He does offer the half measure to me for tasting, which is somewhat appeasing.

"I know Montaña isn't the best area," Luis says as Dek moves away to check on another table. "That's one of the reasons I bring Al with me to work. If someone wants to break in, let them. There's nothing to steal. But Al wouldn't see it that way, and I don't want him to get hurt."

"But why be there at all? You have savings. It doesn't have to be the lap of luxury, but—"

He does this little shrug-slash-smile thing I've never seen him do before. It's a kid gesture, insolent and endearing. "You know, I actually like it there. It's quiet. Sometimes, at night, it feels like I'm the only human alive." He laughs, maybe at himself. "Really, it's not bad. Come see for yourself sometime."

I mean to take just a sip of wine, but I can't stop. I drain the glass. Luis watches, but in the candlelight his expression is unreadable. He pours my refill in silence. I wait until he's done, until he looks at me again. "I don't do repeats," I tell him.

"I made a mistake."

"Just one?"

He grins, but there's no arrogance in it now. "One after another. But here's the thing, Pélagie. Every one of those mistakes—and if I wanted I could trace them all the way to law school, beyond even—they all brought me here. To Al, and to Curaçao. And to you." He reaches across the table, his open hand asking me for—for what? Forgiveness? Acceptance?

I ignore it. "No cheesiness. Please. It's the ultimate insult."

He nods, turns his hand palm down on the table, but leaves it there, invading my space. "I don't want a do-over. I wouldn't take it, except maybe on leaving Al. And I'd do it for him, not for me. These mistakes have been my saving grace. I'd really like it if you could see it that way, too."

I sit back, as far away from that hand as I can without leaving the table. "You were going to London and then you didn't. So. Tell me what happened."

He takes a breath, picks up his wine glass but changes his mind and sets it back down. "Maybe I figured out—you know, really comprehended—the truth of what you told me that day at the condo, the day I asked you to take Al. I made a commitment the day I took him in, whether I knew it or not. Maybe I want to be the kind of man who honors that."

He rubs the side of his cheek and I notice how smooth his skin looks. He must have shaved just before leaving his house. For reasons I'm not prepared to explore, that makes me want to cry.

"Maybe I just got tired of not having roots. I haven't had a home since I left Mexico to go to college—a real home, not just a place to sleep or an address to show off or a custom-made closet for my clothes. I've been a nomad all my adult life. I don't regret it, but... I think maybe I've had enough." And then he ruins it all with his stupid grin. "For now, anyway."

"For now. Right. So how long are you going to do this? Play at this hippie fuck-the-corporate-world shit?"

"I don't know. I—"

"Will you go back to being a lawyer?"

"Maybe. I don't—"

"Will you stay in Curaçao? In that rented Montaña shack? Will you buy a house?"

"I don't know." He holds my gaze, and I see discomfort. Finally.

"What will happen to Al when you get tired of diving, the way you got tired of lawyering?"

"Wherever I go, he goes. China, Timbuktu—"

"What if you get tired of him, too?"

His eyes darken with anger. "What I got tired of was playing a game where every win is a flash in the pan, nothing's enough, ever. I got tired of living by a measuring stick of achievements that mean nothing except to a tiny group of people. I got tired of working my ass off so some rich dudes could cheat their government."

"Oh, I see. And teaching those same rich dudes to dive is so much loftier?"

He finally pulls his hand back to his side of the table. "I didn't leave, Pélagie. I didn't leave Al, and I didn't leave you."

"This was never about me."

"Then why can't you forgive me?"

I hold my wine glass aloft in a toast. "I can, and I have. What I can't do is trust you."

"Because I don't know where I'll be next year, next month?"

"Because you can't be trusted! Because I'm not a dog. Because, hard as I try, I can't live just in the moment. I don't want the future to chew me up and spit me out."

"You were the one who said no one has a lease on the future. Promises are the worst kind of fallacy, remember? Isn't that what you said?"

I need something to swallow, but my glass is dry. Again. Luis beats me to the bottle. His fingers graze mine as he picks it up.

"Come with me to Bonaire next weekend," he says as he pours.

"No."

His eyes never leave the flow of red. "I'll be diving most of the time, even at night, so you won't have to see me much. Maybe just at breakfast. If you're up early enough."

"No."

"The diving people are great. You'll love them."

"I probably know them already."

He slides the glass, a perfect third full, towards me. "Maybe not. Maybe I can still surprise you. And maybe, if you want, we can stay one more day. Just the two of us. I'm off on Mondays."

He's searching my face with that naïve moxie of his.

I take the coward's way out. "I'll think about it," I say.

A lazy afternoon in Bonaire, hammocks, Luis asking me to teach him more ridiculous Dutch expressions. *Now the monkey comes out of the sleeve. They're talking about little cows and little calves.*

Things never go back to the way they were. And perhaps it's for the best. We've no business, none of us, trying to return to the places where we were happy once. All we'll find is blighted hope.

Perhaps all we can do is build anew.

◆

Curaçao is contrast. Clear blue ocean; stark land of cacti and rock. Water and fruit are expensive; gas and cigarettes cheap. Ten political parties; two bookstores. The tragedy of slavery; the joy of *Carnaval*. Jew and Muslim having a soda at the *snék*. The black-and-white couples and their beautiful children of corkscrew curls and eyes of jade. Europe's open mind, Latin America's open heart—both wrapped in Caribbean laid-back.

Dutch houses in Caribbean colors (and refinery smokestacks in the background). Dutch vocabulary at Latin volume with Caribbean cadence. Merengue and tumba and André Hazes. On New Year's Eve, people hug and say cheers at 7.00pm—midnight in Holland—and a Caribbean steel band plays.

To speak two languages is a handicap; to speak only one is a freak show. It's cosmopolitan and provincial, sophisticated and naïve. It's a diorama of the world.

And, for a certain kind of person, it's paradise.

◆

Epilogue
December 31st

I

On the last day of the year, Luis Villalobos is at a moment of flux and flow. Of transfiguration of the spirit, of discovery of his mettle.

Luis is becoming a dog behaviorist.

"So what now?" From the desk, Jan, the dive instructor, looks down at Luis over the bifocals perched on his chirpy nose.

Luis is on the floor of the tiny dive shop office, his back against the display case of snorkel sets and underwater flashlights and t-shirts with the shop's logo, his legs splayed out in front of him. Al is curled on an old towel next to him, all fifty-two kilos of dog crammed into the corner between display case and wall. "We wait."

"Aha. Just, uh, sit and… watch the dog, eh? Exciting stuff, dog training."

"Behavior modification. Not training."

Jan snorts a *whatever rocks your boat* chortle and checks his watch. "It's almost twelve. What do you say we continue your behavior huppeldepupp with a cold Polar?"

"Most constructive thing you've said all day. Let me give you some money."

Jan dismisses him with one swing of his arm and disappears into the glare of the midday sun. When he's gone, Luis reaches over to rub his dog behind the ears. "Where else in the world does drinking at New Year's begin at noon, Al? Bless Curaçao."

Al closes his eyes at the familiar touch, but his tail only wags once, and only at the very tip. The trembling, though, has stopped. For the moment.

The bar out by the dock probably isn't too crowded yet; Jan is back in hardly the time it would take the barman to uncap the bottles of beer. He folds his long frame down to the cool tile next to Luis and hands him one of the Polars. "Gelukkig nieuwjaar."

"Feliz año, cabrón." Luis straightens up to take the beer, and as they touch bottles he says, solemnly, "May you get laid in the new year."

"Klootzak." In a single movement, Jan downs half his beer.

"I know that one. Dick-head, right?"

"No. That's eikel."

"What's this clothes-sack thing, then?"

"Asshole. Sort of."

Not two days ago, on a slow afternoon, Jan gave him an intro course to the art of obscenity in Dutch. He should've taken notes. "Right. Okay. And then I answer—what do I answer?"

"You? You just say thank you, man."

Luis grins. "Cabrón."

"Your repertoire needs work. Klootzak."

Luis might have saved face with a barrage of the choicest, juiciest Mexican insults, the kind that would make a loader in La Merced blush, but what sounds like machine gunfire explodes in the distance, from up by the Jan Sofat hills. "Shit." Luis hands back his beer to Jan. "Here we go."

Nails scrabbling against the tile, Al is squeezing himself deeper into the corner, as if he might, if he tries hard enough, disappear into a parallel dimension and leave this whole wretchedness behind.

Out comes the 2-quart baggie of sausage pieces. What's left of it, after the morning's *pagaras*. All this week they've been going through two, sometimes three, of these baggies a day.

Is it working? Luis isn't sure.

"What's this? Eh, Al? Yummy sausage. Mmm."

He holds a greasy slice under the dog's nose. "Al? Al. Take it, bud. Come on. This is way more interesting than— yeah, that's it." The mouth opens, ever so gently, and takes it. He has another slice ready while the dog is still chewing. And another. And another. Until the din of the *pagara* finally slows then stops. It's a long one, maybe a full five minutes. By the time the echo fades over the bay of Spaanse Water, the baggie's contents are down by half. And, although Al is still hunkered in his corner, his head and ears are up, and his eyes are alert, darting between the baggie and the hand that so conveniently made the stuff available.

"Good boy, Al! Good, good boy!"

"You praise him for wanting more fuckin' German sausage bits." Jan shakes his head. "This dog's achievement bar is low."

Luis wipes his palms on his shorts and holds out a hand, semi-free of sausage grease and dog drool, to get his beer back. "Last week, with the big fireworks at Santa Rosa, he went nuts, man. Out of control. Sausage, liverwurst—he was not interested. He crawled under the bed and howled and howled. Bad. So yeah. This is an achievement."

Jan nods, reaches one hand to stroke Al's neck. "They distract you with food, huh? Sweet."

Luis considers explaining about positive associations, but decides it's a waste. He thought the financial world had shown him the epitome of skepticism, but all those jaded lawyers and accountants have nothing on Jan's absolute faith that seeing is believing—and, unlike Luis, he hasn't seen Pélagie's dogs.

"One more Polar before we close up?" Jan is already standing up.

Luis reaches for Jan's empty. "My turn."

"You're leaving me alone with Al? I'm... honored beyond words."

"Clothes-sack."

"Clothes-what?" Jan cackles. "Oh, you mean kloot-zak."

"What I just fucking said."

"*KLOOTZAK*. Long O. The T isn't silent."

Luis gives him the finger. "Al, stay."

Through his thin cotton t-shirt, the sun outside feels like one of those good, long hugs, the kind that put your soul back together. It's a gorgeous day—aren't they all?—but... It just doesn't feel like the end of the year. The Christmas decorations along the wooden bannisters, the lights hung from thatched roofs, it all looks out of place here in the heat and the salty breeze and stray grains of sand crunching under his flip-flops. And it's bait, for Luis at least, to a weird kind of nostalgia.

His phone buzzes against his leg as he steps up to the bar. At that same moment, in the red bougainvillea at the far edge of the terrace, the peripheries of his vision and his consciousness register a hummingbird. A tiny, magical thing of iridescent green and delicate beak, that seems to be standing still—no, *is* standing, actually standing, its gossamer legs wrapped around one of the sturdier branches.

He's never seen a hummingbird not in flight.

It's so casual, this glimpse, that before he has time to process, his eyes are moving away already, his hands already answering the call. He looks again, all attention this time, but there's only bougainvillea.

And he needs to take this call. "Hey."

"Hi."

One syllable, and all his insides go acrobatic. How long does this feeling last, this irrational pleasure at a voice, a presence? No, not long in his experience, and this time it's already lasted beyond even optimistic expectations. He's done with games of pride and fear, though. He means to enjoy it, to give in to it and live it and savor it, for as long as it chooses to keep him company. "I'm glad you called."

Pélagie laughs. "You may not be, eventually. Are you busy?"

"Nah. Getting a last beer before we close up. What's up?"

"I need a favor. What time will you be home?"

Luis's fantasies of dragons and knights swinging swords kick in. "Are you okay? What do you need?"

"I'd rather ask you in person. Can I come by later? Would you mind?"

"No, of course. Yes. Please."

"I warn you, this isn't a pleasure call."

He feels the heat of a blush—a blush! Luis Villalobos, thirty-nine going on thirteen!—climbing up his neck. "Anything involving you is pleasure. For me."

"What time should I come by?" They make her uncomfortable, these Latin displays of emotion, but he thinks he hears a smile in her voice.

"I can be home in fifteen minutes."

"There's no rush."

"Of course there is."

She laughs. "I'm going to hang up now. See you—"

In his best Pepe Aguilar (which really isn't that good), he begins to sing. "Por mujeres como tú—"

"No, no. Luis, please."

The bartender looks up, one eyebrow raised. Luis winks at him and carries on. "—amor, hay hombres como yo, que se pueden morir—"

"Oh, god."

"—por dignidad mordiendo el corazón..."

The line is dead. The bartender, though, is grinning.

II

Luis's cleaning lady quit the week before Christmas. Sherman, the neighbor, says it's because she wanted to go home for the holidays. "E ta Colombiana, no?" he'd asked, in the aggravated tone of someone being forced to state the obvious. To Luis, however, why being Colombian required quitting remained a mystery. Couldn't she just tell the people she cleans for that she'd be back in January?

Firecrackers—pops and whistles of solo detonations, the war zone racket of the *pagara* ropes—sound intermittently, but Al, aside from ears pulled back and a meek hunkering of his shoulders, is calm. Could be because none sound too close. Could be the car ride; he loves the Suzuki Jimny Luis bought—not second-hand, more like fourth—mainly, Luis suspects, because there's no roof on the back. Or maybe the positive-association thing is working. Whatever the explanation, the dog follows Luis around as he attacks the clutter in the living room, runs a hot sinkful of water in the kitchen to soak three dishes and a greasy pan, stuffs onto already overflowing closet shelves the two clear plastic bags of clothes he picked up last week from the Chinese *wasserette* down the street. He should get a washing machine, but—let's face it, the only difference will be he'll have mounds of dirty clothes instead of stacked bags of clean, nicely folded ones.

When did he become so messy? It's not just the clothes or the dog hair or the dust on every surface—including the vacuum cleaner. And it's not the MIA maid's fault, either.

He's lived alone for twenty years, more often than not without housekeeping, and his pads were always spotless. Maybe a bit too spotless, too far up on the Architectural Digest scale of un-lived-in-ness.

Then again, he didn't really live them *in*, did he?

He's tucking in a clean set of sheets around the mattress—hopeful, always hopeful—when he hears the crunch of tires on gravel outside, and Al is off down the hall, nails scrabbling, and doing that funny yap-howl he reserves for his favorite people.

"It's open," he calls out from the hallway. "Come on in."

Pélagie is scratching Al's jaw through the fence. She looks up, motions with her free hand to her Explorer's rolled-down windows. "The car's open."

"So close it." But he starts down the walk to the gate. *This is not a pleasure call.* A frisson of alarm begins a slow drip into his bloodstream.

"Hi," she says when he opens the gate, and stands on tiptoe to give him a much too hurried kiss, then walks to the other side of her car. He follows; what else? But the drip is now an all-out leak.

Pélagie puts an arm into the back seat. "Remember her?"

A light-brown face peeks out at him, made even smaller by the huge doe eyes that squint in the glare and blink at him then at Pélagie then back at him. It takes him a moment, longer than it should have. It's been—what, two weeks? ten days?—since that frustrated beach day. Driving up to Banda Abou, passing the Selikor garbage dump, Pélagie telling him to stop, digging her fingers into his arm. The smell of garbage floating into the car as she got out.

"Selli—no, Sella. Right?" The vet's receptionist spelled it *Cella*. He laughed with Pélagie about that afterwards, their female cello. "Hey, Sella. Wow, look at her fur. She's gorgeous. You couldn't even tell she had that white star on her chest."

"She needs a bath."

"Another one? No, she's—"

There is a pleading in the way Pélagie lifts her eyes to him. Discreet and reserved, but there nonetheless. "I think today's the day."

She doesn't look too skinny, he'd said the day they found her. But Pélagie was already climbing back in, the dog in her arms. *Because she's pregnant.* They spent an hour at the vet, who confirmed puppies were indeed on the way and it was too late to do anything about it. Pélagie acted as if that were tragic, but Luis was secretly relieved. Poor puppies.

He just never imagined he'd be the midwife in attendance.

No. Impossible. "Pélagie, I've never—I don't—"

"All she needs is a quiet, sheltered space away from other dogs. You know that's not doable at my place. Especially today. You wouldn't have to do anything."

"There must be other places. Other people. I mean, what about Al? And I'd have no clue…"

Pélagie is looking at Sella, stroking the dog's head through the open window, so it seems as if she's talking to her instead of him. "There's no one else."

He knew that. She wouldn't be here unless this was her absolute last option, for the simple reason that it's a bad option. He's completely inexperienced, he'd be on the phone to her every five minutes. He'd be in a panic at the first sight of blood. Pélagie knows this about him. He can't for the life of him imagine why she would—

Unless she's going to stay with Sella. With him.

Hope swirls in, and in its hit-of-heroin rush he senses an impending and inescapable shift of the things he takes for granted.

123

III

They make love in the shade of the back porch, the papery rustle of palm leaves above them in the mid-afternoon heat. In the slow coming to after orgasm, for reasons unknowable, he remembers the hummingbird.

"I saw a hummingbird today."

Pélagie, curled up against his chest, says nothing. He can't see her face; maybe she's dozing. He wouldn't hear her over the wind and the hum of his bloodstream anyway.

"He was standing still. I've never seen that before. Just... standing, on a branch. Like—I don't know, like he was taking a break or something."

She turns her head and kisses the underside of his chin, but her eyes stay closed. "Maybe he was tired."

"I don't think so. It was more... relaxed, somehow. His attitude."

"His attitude?" She smiles, and he looks in awe at how beautiful her mouth is like that, parting, widening.

"Yeah. He just seemed... to be contemplating."

She looks at him now. "Contemplating what?"

He touches a finger to the corner of her lips, traces them once, twice. "I don't know. He didn't look nervous, or twitchy. He stood tall, not looking around or anything. Just... Yeah. Contemplating."

"The Contemplative Hummingbird, huh?" Her smile becomes an all-out grin, but there's sweetness in her eyes. "Okay."

"I could be wrong."

"Or you could be right." She stretches to reach his lips, lingers for a moment, then sits up. "I'm going to check on Sella."

He pulls a throw pillow under his head, makes himself comfortable. "I'll hold the fort here. Hey, would you check on Al, too?"

After the obligatory rounds of sniffing, Sella—who established a wide personal space around Al, and enforced it with growls and snaps that left no room for dialogue—settled into the spare bedroom. Al, his friendliness chastised but not quite curbed, set up guard outside the closed door, every now and then touching his oversized nose to the crack at the bottom. The growl he got from the other side didn't faze him. Even when a *pagara* started up, closer by this time, he stayed put.

He's still there, apparently; Luis hears Pélagie talking to him just before the bedroom door opens (squeak) and closes (thud).

"Hey, Al?" he calls into the house. "Why don't you come out here, guy? Sella's not interested, buddy."

Nothing. Maybe tail thumping, faint, but no nails clicking on tile.

"Have it your way, bud. I'm going to—"

"Luis? Luis!" A squeak, a thud, then the whispery footsteps of Pélagie running barefoot. When she bursts out onto the porch, excitement is all over her face. "They're coming. The puppies!"

Oh, boy. Puppies, about to be born under his roof. Messy, probably. He hopes he won't have to mop up blood tomorrow. Or the day after. How long does it take, anyway? He's heard of women in labor for twenty hours, forty. If Pélagie's going to be here two days, he should probably call Jan and ask for—

"Aren't you coming?" Pélagie is standing in the door again. Waiting. For him.

"I thought you said you didn't need help."

"I don't. But you've never seen a birth."

And I'd like to keep it that way. "Oh. Uh, well. I think I better not. You know, me and blood——"

"Don't be such a pussy. Besides, there's no blood. Not a lot, anyway."

"I really don't think——"

"Fine. No, no worries." She disappears inside, then calls out from the hallway, "Chicken."

Which is fine, too. A real man knows his limitations. The boundaries he cannot cross, shouldn't cross, even in the face of shameless manipulation.

With a sigh, he sits up. Bullshit.

And then there's the hummingbird. Incredibly still, and yet, in its stillness, vibrantly, electrically alive. What would it be like, to be that bird? To have the power of flight and the potential for speed, and yet possess the willpower to harness them, even momentarily, and *stand still?*

He's not sure what it means, or why his throat closes when he thinks about this too much. But, somehow, Sella and her puppies are mixed in it.

He pulls on his shorts, shuffles into his flip-flops (for the blood, just in case there is some), and walks into the house.

On FATCA and Other Tax Issues
Author's Note

The Foreign Account Tax Compliance Act (FATCA) entered into United States law in 2010. The objective of its provisions is the reporting of financial assets held outside the US by US residents.

The US is one of only two countries in the world (the other is Eritrea) to have a worldwide system of taxation. While other countries are concerned only with income sourced in their territory, residents of the US must declare all their income, regardless of its source, to US tax authorities.

Since the system's introduction (in the early days of the American Civil War), US residents have tried to skirt this obligation by placing assets offshore. Caribbean jurisdictions provided enticing options, as did several European countries (Switzerland comes to mind). But the IRS was never far behind.

In the last twenty years, international pressure and growing economic globalization have persuaded all but the most rebellious offshore jurisdictions into cooperating with revenue authorities. And the strictures imposed on US residents with offshore investments have made American clients increasingly undesirable for fiduciary service providers. The withholding logistics are, quite simply, a nightmare that only very few are willing, and have the staff and know-how, to take on.

FATCA is only the latest of these strictures. But it's special in one important aspect: before FATCA, the burden of compliance with US tax requirements rested exclusively on the US taxpayer. Since 2010, however, that burden has been broadened to include service providers.

Simply stated, under FATCA regulations, any intermediary anywhere in the world—Caribbean fiduciary, European banker, British trustee, etc.—who provides services to residents of the United States with bank and/or investment accounts in other countries is obligated to disclose this information to the IRS (via any of the applicable forms, and for any of the applicable amounts).

For the purpose of these stories, I've played a bit fast and loose with details where FATCA is concerned. The agreement binding Curaçao to FATCA provisions only came into effect in December 2014, long after these stories were written and published as part of Pure Slush's *2014 A Year In Stories* project. Therefore, the deadlines, consequences, and requirements of FATCA as described in this book may not represent the specific reality of what the actual agreement would entail for a financial institution such as (the entirely fictional) Ehrlich Fiduciary.

Acknowledgments

No story is an island, and this one owes much to many.

Publisher Matt Potter invited me to join his *2014 A Year in Stories* project and spent countless hours bringing Luis Villalobos to life—and then, as if that wasn't already awesomeness enough, he agreed to publish Luis's stories as a single volume, and spent another good chunk of this year weeding out the purple prose that snuck into our revised versions while I slept. (It wasn't me, Matt.) For all this and for his everlasting good humor (and outstanding cover designs), Matt is—as we're fond of saying in Mexico—going to heaven shoes and all.

For inspiration, expertise, and all-out support: Friends in the financial industry (who, for their own safety, have requested to remain—no, I jest) helped with plot points and clarifications. Accuracy is theirs, mistakes are mine. Dive instructor Hans Pleij, whose life exemplifies living the dream, and his skill has forever ruined me for any other diving outfit. (Note: he's not from Amsterdam.) Randal Corsen, musician and composer extraordinaire and generous of expertise. More generosity from Carolina Gomes-Casseres and Suzy del Valle; the book's New York launch wouldn't have happened without you. Fellow writers at the Internet Writing Workshop invariably provided brilliant feedback, draft after draft.

When it came time for blurbs, I wrote to my favorite authors—and they not just responded but made time in their busy schedules for *Miracle* and me. My gratitude is boundless.

This story wouldn't have even begun, however, if not for Cor Zwartveld. He's not a writer, he's not an editor; he's my partner and my best friend, and he might have had no clue whether what I wrote was any good, but he believed in me so thoroughly that I had no choice but to believe in me, too. Masha danki, dushi. Voor alles.

About the Author

Guilie Castillo Oriard is a Mexican writer and dog rescuer living in Curaçao. She misses Mexican food and Mexican *amabilidad*, but the laissez-faire attitude (and the beaches) are fair exchange. And the bounty of cultural diversity provides great fodder for her obsession with culture clashes.

Her work has appeared online (http://pureslush.webs.com/authorsc.htm#825261724) and, in print, as part of *gorge: a novel in stories (Pure Slush Vol. 4)* and the twelve *2014 A Year in Stories* volumes.

She's currently working on her first novel, and blogs at http://guilie-castillo-oriard.blogspot.com.

The Miracle of Small Things is her first solo book.

Books from *Truth Serum Press*

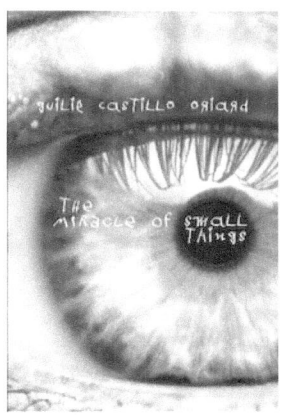

The Miracle of Small Things
978-1-925101-73-7 (paperback)
978-1-925101-74-4 (eBook)

La Ronde
978-1-925101-64-5 (paperback)
978-1-925101-65-2 (eBook)

Based on True Stories
978-1-925101-75-1 (paperback)
978-1-925101-76-8 (eBook)

Visit the *Truth Serum Press* catalogue online
http://truthserumpress.net/catalogue/

www.ingramcontent.com/pod-product-compliance
Lightning Source LLC
Chambersburg PA
CBHW021425200626
46814CB00015B/1481